Ellie
& the
Bunheads

SALLY WARNER

Alfred A. Knopf ✏️ New York

*I thank my son Andrew Blight, currently with the
Pittsburgh Ballet, for his suggestions and technical help.
I thank Philip Fuller, Charles Fuller, and Cynthia Young
for allowing me to be a fly on the wall for so many years
at Le Studio and the Pasadena Dance Theatre.
I also thank Jayn Hunter, M.S.W., for her valuable
assistance. Any mistakes are, of course, my own.*

THIS IS A BORZOI BOOK PUBLISHED BY ALFRED A. KNOPF, INC.

Copyright © 1997 by Sally Warner
Jacket art courtesy of Giraudon/Art Resource, NY
Edgar Degas: *The Dance Foyer at the Opera on Rue le Peletier*
All rights reserved under International and Pan-American Copyright Conventions.
Published in the United States of America by Alfred A. Knopf, Inc., New York,
and simultaneously in Canada by Random House of Canada Limited, Toronto.
Distributed by Random House, Inc., New York.
http://www.randomhouse.com/

Library of Congress Cataloging-in-Publication Data
Warner, Sally.
Ellie and the bunheads / by Sally Warner
p.   cm.
Summary: Thirteen-year-old Ellie explores the ups and
downs of becoming a serious ballet dancer and a teenager.
ISBN 0-679-88229-4 (trade)
ISBN 0-679-98229-9 (lib. bdg.)
[1. Ballet dancing—Fiction.] I. Title.
PZ7.W24644E1   1997
[Fic]—dc20   96-26192

Printed in the United States of America
10 9 8 7 6 5 4 3 2 1

For Andrew, who has taught me so much about courage—
and about being an artist

Contents

Well, first there's the question of my rear end, if I'm going to be perfectly honest about my body. Which I have to be, if I really want to be a dancer. My rear end, my bottom, my behind. Let's face it—my butt! Oh, it's okay for the time being, but it will probably be my worst feature someday. If your rear end even is a feature. What should I do now to keep it from dragging on the floor in a few years? That would be so gross. I know, no more peanut butter. And I don't even like peanut butter very much, so no biggie. But at least it's a start toward advance self-improvment.

—To be continued.

1 Ellie's Rear End

The silver-topped cane whizzed straight down toward the ground as if it were a butcher's knife. It passed only a few inches from Ellie Lane's rear end. "Leticia Elena, hold in some of that hamburger!" the tiny ballet teacher said.

Ellie—L. E. being the natural abbreviation for Leticia Elena, the fancy name she hated—gritted her teeth and tried to do as Ms. Hawkins directed without sticking out her stomach. The big droop was starting already, she thought, grim. She looked at the wall-length mirror in front of her as she completed her grands battements, those big, sideways kicks this class always ended with. She saw Ms. Hawkins pause behind Bella, whose rear end stuck out most of the time. Bella—Arabella Amory—had changed ballet schools the previous September, and she and Ellie had slowly become friends, though only at the dance studio so far.

But Ms. Hawkins didn't mention Bella's bottom today. "Arabella, we're not kicking field goals," she said instead. "Keep your back straight, dear."

Ellie saw Bella bite her lower lip as she tried to straighten up, kick high, and look serene—all at the same time. Ballet was hard! Ellie tried to relax her own mouth, just in case she looked as anxious as her friend.

"Beautiful arms, Dawn, not basketball hoops," Ms. Hawkins said, moving on to the next girl.

Dawn looked as though she was going to cry; her brimming eyes fixed on the mirror in front of her. The least little criticism lately and she fell apart, Ellie thought. She sure had changed.

Ellie had first noticed it about a year ago: Dawn had started looking tired a lot of the time then, and she'd begun asking girls in the ballet dressing room if they thought she looked sick, if they thought she had a fever.

Weird, Ellie thought.

Ellie had known Dawn since preschool. Their mothers had always been friends, but had Ellie and Dawn ever really liked each other? Well, maybe when they were little. She kind of remembered sitting opposite Dawn on a teeter-totter once, and laughing. That was a long time ago, though. They hadn't laughed much lately.

And now that Dawn had started losing her temper so frequently, and bursting into tears for no reason, she sure wasn't getting any easier to be around.

Ellie sighed and tried to relax her hand. She and Dawn were just so different these days. Maybe that's why they got on each other's nerves.

Now Mrs. Fiori, the class pianist, was playing her final chords. "And one," Ms. Hawkins said as the class made deep curtsies toward Mrs. Fiori's corner, "and two." The class curtsied to Ms. Hawkins. There was the usual polite spatter of applause from the perspiring dancers as they all walked toward the door; that was traditional in ballet. Ms. Hawkins—who looked perfect, as usual, despite having energetically demonstrated all the day's combinations to her class—led the way into the lobby, black chiffon scarf floating behind her.

Ellie joined the dancers leaving the studio, their hair pulled back in buns, their feet turned out from years of training. And once again, she wondered if she really and truly was one of them.

Or if she *wasn't* a real bunhead, would she ever be able to quit?

It wasn't that she didn't *like* ballet. Ellie poked her feet through the holes at the bottom of her pale pink tights and then rolled the tights up around her ankles. She slipped reddened feet into her worn sneakers. No, she loved it. The by-now-familiar combination of music, hard work, and concentration made the ballet studio feel like home to her—no, she thought, better than home.

The trouble was, her mother seemed to love ballet even more than Ellie did. She loved it too much, if possible—considering that Ellie was the one who was doing all the dancing.

Ellie had heard the story a hundred times. Her mom had been a child who loved beautiful things—art, music, and especially dance. She had lived way out in western Pennsylvania, though, in a mining town. She could have taken tap or baton twirling, but no: once she had seen the ballerina Margot Fonteyn dance *Swan Lake* on public television, that had been that.

Forever after, Ellie's mom had called the famous dancer "Miss Fonteyn," as though she'd been her very own teacher or something, and had often praised the ballet star's sleek, dark beauty. Yes, it was ballet or nothing for Ellie's mother after that, which Ellie had also heard her mom say a hundred times.

But ballet lessons had not been available in such a small town. That's why Ellie was so lucky to live in a big city like Philadelphia, her mother never failed to add at this point.

Ellie always felt sad when she heard the next part of the story: her mother had been forced to put away her wish to dance. She did this the way someone else might have hung a sparkly new dress in the back of a closet, having missed the party.

4

Instead of dancing, her mom had consoled herself by looking at pictures in the best art books in the town's library and listening to the most beautiful music she could find on the radio. Those things were within her reach at least, she'd often told Ellie. And that was how she had been able to keep at least some of the beauty she craved in her life, for a while anyway.

Ellie's mother's story always rushed along from there: that young girl had grown up, gotten married, and moved to the city, much to her delight. She had started working in the beauty salon that she now owned. And then beautiful Leticia Elena—*Ellie*—had been born. That's how she finished her story, every single time.

The end, Ellie's mom would say, giving her daughter a hug.

Mrs. Lane had enrolled her young daughter in preballet when she was only five. At eight, when she started Level One, Ellie had been taking one ballet class a week. She didn't mind that. After a year she was promoted to the next level, which made her feel as though she was climbing a ladder. But to where?

By the time she was ten, Ellie was taking three ballet classes a week. Her mother had been thrilled at the progress Ellie was making, and that made Ellie proud. It was nice being good at something.

Her dad had started having problems at work about that time, and things weren't going so great for him with her mom, either—not from what Ellie could gather. A few times a year, her parents would have a huge fight behind their closed bedroom door. Then they would emerge as if nothing at all had happened.

But Ellie's dad seemed happy enough the rest of the time. And her mom was happy when Ellie was dancing well.

So it all worked out.

Still, sometimes Ellie had felt restless, bored with her routine. "Why can't I take ice-skating lessons, too?" she'd asked once.

"Ellie, you may only be ten, but you're a born dancer," her mother had said back then. "You're good, honey—you don't want to risk hurting yourself on the ice. And if you want to keep on improving in ballet, you can't go spreading yourself thin doing a whole bunch of other things."

Mrs. Lane's voice had been low, serious, as if she were talking to a girlfriend. Ellie liked it when they talked like that, just the two of them. "I guess not," she had told her mother reluctantly.

"And anyway," her mom had added, "do you have any idea what ice-skating lessons would cost? In addition to all that dance?"

That was another thing—the money. Now, Ellie was twelve years old, and she was taking four ballet classes a week. Her lessons already cost the Lanes a lot of money; Ellie knew her mom and dad worked hard so she could keep on dancing. There was no room in the budget for a lot of extra treats.

The cost made it hard to complain, but sometimes Ellie *felt* like complaining: about all the time she spent taking class, about her aching feet, about being tired. But usually she bit her lip and kept quiet.

Still, the look in her parents' eyes when they saw her dance—well, the look in her mother's eyes, anyway—made Ellie swallow hard sometimes. It was such a hungry look, as though Mrs. Lane was eating up every turn, every jump, every single beautiful movement Ellie made. Her mother never seemed to get full, though.

But I really do love ballet, Ellie reassured herself. If her mom loved it too—so what?

There was nothing wrong with that, was there?

"Ellie?" a soft voice was murmuring in her ear. "Did you hear me?" It was Bella, who by now had struggled into her navy school sweatshirt. Bella went to private school. Her oval face shone damp and pink above the school's crest.

"Hmm?" Ellie said.

"I was just asking if you were going to try out for the company." The Philadelphia Dance Theater was a company made up of the best dance students in the entire city. They performed locally throughout the year and took part in regional dance competitions. Tryouts were once a year, the last week in May, and they had been the main topic of conversation among the girls in Level Six for weeks. You had to be thirteen to try out.

"Oh, I don't know," Ellie said. "I might." Her mom obviously wanted her to audition and acted as though there was no question about it, which was driving Ellie nuts.

"You mean you're not sure?" Bella sounded as if she couldn't believe her ears. "But you're so good!"

Dawn Upjohn flexed a narrow foot and gave an inelegant sniff. "You have to be *more* than good, Arabella. You have to really want it, too. You have to be hungry for it," she added dramatically, as if quoting from a magazine article. She cast a significant glance at Bella's rounded stomach as she spoke. Bella blushed even pinker than usual.

Ellie could tell that Dawn was still angry about getting that correction in class, and she was taking it out on Bella. "Oh, I don't know," she argued. "I mean, look at Anne Marie." Anne Marie Leone was a high school girl who had been in the company for two years already. She was famous for appearing to be bored—with everything.

"Anne Marie can act any way she wants," Dawn said with a shrug. "Like you said, just look at her. She's got the perfect body, *and* she's beautiful. Lucky!"

"She's also a good dancer," Ellie pointed out, "and that's not luck, that's work."

"It sure is," Bella agreed, and she sighed.

"So, *Leticia*," Dawn said, ignoring Bella, "what about it? Are you auditioning?"

"Look, I said I don't know!" Ellie was angry. She hated being called Leticia, and Dawn knew it.

Ellie had only been five when she'd taken her first dance class, though, and when the teacher had said, "Stand up straight, Leticia Elena," Ellie hadn't corrected her. How do you correct a grownup who is giving you a correction? Ellie got mixed up just thinking about it. So that had been that, for the next seven years.

"Oh, come on. Of course you know if you'll audition or not," Dawn said, clearly not believing Ellie.

Ellie turned to face Bella. "Are *you* going to try out?" she asked. Bella ducked her head, which meant yes, but she looked nervous.

Dawn laughed as she got up. "Money can't buy everything," she observed to no one in particular. She slung her dance bag over her shoulder and left.

Bella's face wasn't pink any longer; it was pale.

"Hey, come on, she wasn't talking to you," Ellie said. "And anyway, consider the source."

"But why does she hate me so much?" Bella asked helplessly. "She barely even knows me."

Ellie shrugged. "She's been really moody lately. Remember when she yelled at Heather in the dressing room last week, for no reason? And then cried? But I'm sure she didn't mean what she said to you."

"Yes, she did *too* mean it," Bella answered, stubborn for once. "And she's right—I don't have a prayer of getting in the company, not even with that coach."

"With what coach?" Ellie asked.

"My mother is paying this lady to coach me now," Bella said, embarrassed. "She thinks it will help me in the audition."

"You're kidding. You mean you're taking private lessons?"

"Yeah, but worse. She's going to start videotaping me

and everything. So there I'll be for all eternity, clomping around on pointe for my future grandchildren to see, and for nothing. What a joke," Bella added bitterly.

"But—but doesn't all that videotaping and coaching cost a fortune?" Ellie asked. She knew Arabella's family was rich, but ballet was already plenty expensive, what with four classes a week and pointe shoes at more than fifty dollars a pair. Those shoes didn't last long, either.

"Yeah, but I'm worth it," Bella said with a toss of her head, imitating a television commercial. Her blond curls bounced, but she wasn't smiling.

"Well, good luck," Ellie said, grinning.

"Oh, Ellie, get real," Bella said. She sounded angry now. Ellie had never heard Bella get mad before. "It's like you told Dawn," Bella continued. "Luck has nothing to do with it. And it's like Dawn said, money can't buy everything. The trouble is, I already know that, and so does Daddy, I think. It's my mother who still has to find it out. She acts like it's her right to have a daughter in the company—and she always gets her way. So I'll have to go through with this whole pathetic nightmare like there's really some chance, just for her."

"Maybe—maybe the coach will help, somehow. Maybe you *will* get in, Bella," Ellie said.

Bella looked at her, disappointed. "Don't you turn on me too," she said. "You're the smartest girl here, Ellie. I thought I could count on you to be honest, at least."

"How do you like the vegetarian lasagna, sweetie?" Ellie's mother asked at dinner that night.

"It's great, Mom," Ellie lied. She liked her mother's old recipe better—the one with meat and lots of cheese. But the recipe had changed right after Valentine's Day, when Mrs. Lane hadn't been able to zip up her skirt. Ellie would rather eat a little of the old lasagna than a lot of this.

Her father poked glumly at his dinner. "I thought zucchini only grew in the summer," he said.

"You have to know where to *look*," his wife said. "Now, we have fresh fruit for dessert, so finish up, everyone."

"I think I'm done," Ellie said. "I'll clear the table."

"I know I'm done," Mr. Lane said. "I think I'll skip dessert tonight and go out for a walk." He patted his stomach, indicating how much he needed the exercise. He got up and left the room. A few seconds later, the front door clicked shut.

He was going out for a cheese steak, Ellie thought with a pang of hunger. She sympathized with him; something about her mother's new cooking made her want to go crazy in the other direction too. She now craved fries, hamburgers, cookies.

But her dad probably would have gone out anyway, Ellie admitted to herself. For the past two years, he and her mom had been doing everything possible to avoid one another. Oh, they weren't actually fighting as much as they had when Ellie was ten—not that Ellie knew of, at least—but their strained politeness was almost worse.

Ellie scraped the dinner plates and put them in the sink to soak while her mother sliced cantaloupe and pineapple into two bowls. "This will be delicious," Mrs. Lane promised.

Ellie didn't reply, but she scowled down at the soapy water. It was weird, she thought, but she really used to like fruit, until her mom had started yakking about how good it was for her. Now all she could think about for dessert was ice cream.

"So, sweetie, tell me about class today," her mom said, carrying the two bowls to the table.

Ellie knew her mother meant ballet, rather than any of the classes she was taking at Ben Franklin Middle School. "It was okay," she said, knowing that her mother wanted more details. It was hard to think of any, though. Most ballet classes were about the same. Anyway, did her mom have to know everything?

"Who taught class?"

"Ms. Hawkins. As usual," Ellie said.

"And how did you do?"

"Fine, I guess," Ellie said. She sure wasn't going to mention the correction about her big old rear end sticking out. No question—she'd be eating celery and water for the next month if her mom heard that.

"Any news about the audition?" her mother asked, spearing a chunk of cantaloupe with her fork.

Ellie chewed some pineapple slowly while she tried to come up with a safe reply. "No," she said finally. "Just who's going to try out, and so on."

"Well, I heard from your friend Dawnie's mother before dinner," Ellie's mother said, looking important.

Ellie wondered once more why her mom and Mrs. Upjohn kept up this fantasy that she and Dawn were friends. It was pathetic. "What did she want?" Ellie asked.

"Oh, just to give me her version of who will get into the company. She says you've been doing beautifully, Ellie."

Some of the ballet moms made a big deal out of saying how well other kids were doing in class—face-to-face anyway. Mrs. Upjohn came to watch class every so often, though Ms. Hawkins didn't encourage it. Ellie's mom never could, thank goodness, because of her job.

"She says Dawnie's having trouble with her extension, though," Mrs. Lane said cozily. That was another part of the game some moms played, Ellie had noticed—pretending to be critical of their own kid.

"Oh, Dawn always says that, too," Ellie said, "but she barely wobbles at all."

"Viv says poor Michelle Lewis can't even try out. She's still twelve, did you know that? Of course, her turnout has never been all that hot . . ."

Turnout again—the training of a dancer's body to be an open instrument, as Ms. Hawkins put it. Turnout was most obviously indicated by the feet. In first position, for instance, the heels met, but the toes formed a V—turning out—rather than pointing straight ahead. That's what caused ballet dancers' duck walks, Ellie had come to realize.

"Well, Mom, I'm still only twelve," she pointed out.

"But you'll be thirteen in two weeks. Just think—my baby a teenager!"

"Mmm," Ellie said.

"And Viv said she thought Arabella Amory was going to try out," Ellie's mother continued. She laughed a little, then said, "Honestly! I don't know when that woman's going to quit."

"Who?"

"Mrs. Amory. I mean, obviously she bought that poor girl's way into Level Six last fall by donating all that money to the Philadelphia Dance Theater, but getting her into the company is a different matter entirely."

Ellie had heard her mother complain about Bella and Mrs. Amory before, ever since Bella had switched ballet schools, in fact, but she didn't understand why. It was almost as though Mrs. Lane was jealous of Arabella's mom. But that was crazy, because she didn't even know Mrs. Amory. Not *really*.

"Mom, Mrs. Amory didn't buy Bella's way into anything," Ellie said now. "It doesn't work like that. And anyway, there's nothing wrong with Bella's dancing."

"That's very kind of you, sweetie, but I think we both know what I'm talking about." Mrs. Lane looked down at her stomach as if sending a coded message.

"Her weight, right?" Ellie said bluntly. Her mom had such a thing about weight, Ellie thought. What was that all about? Nobody wanted to be fat, but why be so critical of other people? And how would her mom act if Ellie was the one gaining weight? "Well, I don't think Bella's all that fat," Ellie said. "She could maybe lose five pounds—"

"Or ten," her mother said, teasing.

"Okay, maybe. But she's pretty, Mom. *Really*," Ellie insisted. "Bella looks like one of those old-fashioned paintings in the museum. Not the gigantic ladies, the romantic ones. And she's smart, too—and funny." Ellie was talking faster and faster, as though she could convince her mother that way. Ellie *liked* Bella. "Bella keeps up with everyone in Level Six, Mom, and she's probably more musical than anyone. She really feels the music."

"I appreciate your loyalty to a friend," Mrs. Lane said. "But you're a much better dancer than she is, darling, no matter how much money the Amorys have. And I'm only saying I don't think Arabella's mother should put her daughter through the ordeal of auditioning when that poor girl doesn't have a prayer."

"And what about me?" Ellie asked, feeling rebellious. "Do *I* have a prayer of getting in?"

"Don't be silly—of course you have. Unless you do something ridiculous, of course." And Mrs. Lane laughed at the very idea.

And what about my arms? Can arms be too skinny? Well, at least they're not fat—not yet, anyway. I'll have to watch it, though. But I don't want them to ever look all pumped up, like I'm this truck driver or something. More advance self-improvement: I'll stop eating cookies. Not that there are ever any cookies around here anymore. And I won't carry books in my arms, I'll always use a backpack—maybe that will help. Forget my armpits...too weird-looking and disgusting to even mention.

—To be continued.

2
Ellie's Arms

Ellie stretched and glanced at the clock: ten-thirty already. By the time she got home from dance, ate dinner, and did her homework, it was usually this late. She always felt tired in the morning, and she hated getting up early for school—especially in the winter.

But it was the end of April now, and it had been a warm day. Getting up would be a little easier tomorrow. She shut her math book and shifted in her chair, sore.

Ellie got up and stood in front of her open closet

door: the Lanes lived in an old apartment building on Pine Street, and there was a full-length beveled mirror inside each of the many closets. Ellie hoisted her nightgown and turned sideways to get a better view of her profile.

Nothing stuck out too much, she was relieved to see. She tilted her hips to make her rear end stick out more, then she bulged out her stomach on purpose. She squinted her eyes, trying to imagine how Ms. Hawkins would react. *Hold in some of that hamburger,* she'd probably say.

Ellie turned a little more and tried to get a really good look. She was white, white, *white!* Those girls in magazines—the ones wearing thong bikinis—how did they get so tan, anyway? Ellie giggled, imagining going down to the shore with her parents in the summer. She would take off her T-shirt, peel off her shorts, and—ta-da!—there would be this blinding white glare. Imagine her parents' surprise. . . .

She would probably have to perform CPR on them. And think of the sunburn!

Ellie let her nightgown drop, and she lifted her bare arms up to fifth position, arms low. How did they look—like a basketball hoop? No, her fifth was pretty good. Ellie thought of the sag under her mother's upper arms and hoped guiltily that her own arms would never look like that. So far, so good.

Dawn's arms were okay too, and so was her fifth low, Ellie had to admit. Ms. Hawkins must have just been looking for something to criticize. She did that sometimes, when she was having a bad day.

Anne Marie's arms were beautiful. The girls in Level Six watched company class whenever they could. They always did this silently and with great attention, not only to technique but to style—style in warm-up clothes, makeup, everything. The girls watched Anne Marie more carefully than they did any of the others.

Anne Marie Leone was almost hypnotic in her perfection. Ellie thought of her arms as the perfect dancer's arms: slender, flawless, well modeled without being overly muscular. When she danced, her arms were the most beautiful extension of her body imaginable. Ellie could always imagine a perfect invisible line extending from the older girl's fingertips to the frayed satin toe of her pointe shoe. Ellie thought that someday she wanted to look like that when she danced. She wanted her every movement to seem like the only one possible.

But now it was time for bed.

The cafeteria at Ben Franklin Middle School was always a zoo at lunchtime. Ellie packed her own meal each morning, under her mother's supervision—usually yogurt, a sack of granola, and an apple—but she usually bought skim milk at school. "You need the calcium, not the fat," her mother was always saying. "And don't go eating any junk after school, either." Ellie took a seat at the end of a long, sticky table.

This was her first year at Ben Franklin. The

crowded, constantly changing classes and her own busy after-school schedule meant that she had only been able to get to know a few other girls. They had different lunch periods, though, and so Ellie sometimes ended up eating alone.

Sixth-graders at Ben Franklin were the lowest of the low, but by now—April—they blended in and almost felt they belonged at the school. At least they didn't feel so raw, so new, anymore. Ellie was already starting to look forward to next year, when she would be a seventh-grader—right in the middle. That would be perfect, she thought: there would be no pressure from being either the youngest or the oldest in school.

"Hey, Ellie," someone said. "Can I sit here?" It was Ned Ryan, her friend from math class and chess club.

"Oh—sure," Ellie said.

Ned scooted his chair in across the speckled, sticky floor and pulled a bulging lunch sack from his backpack. Ellie watched him sideways as he carefully arranged his meal in front of him: chicken, a container of pasta salad, celery sticks, an orange, a brownie, and three napkins. He had bought a carton of orange juice at the cafeteria. He sighed happily and started in on the chicken.

"Did you finish your math?" Ellie asked, sprinkling more granola on top of her yogurt. Her stomach growled a little.

"Mmm-hmm," Ned said, nodding. He took a swig of the orange juice and wiped his fingers. His faded blue flannel shirt looked as though it had just been ironed. "It wasn't too bad, was it?" he asked.

"Not once you memorized the equation. My mind kept wandering, though."

"Mine too. It was kind of boring, once you got the hang of it. You going to chess after school?" Ned asked. He, Ellie, and Case Hill, a friend of theirs, were the only sixth-grade members of Ben Franklin's after-school chess club. It met on Thursday afternoons, but sometimes it was hard for Ellie to go. Even though the Level Six ballet classes met Mondays, Wednesdays, Fridays, and Saturdays, the girls were sometimes asked to come in at other times to rehearse for special events.

But Ellie didn't talk to Ned or Case much about dance. It's not that she thought they would tease her about it, because they never would. It was more that dance was too important to her—and her feelings about it too complicated—for her to discuss it while gobbling granola. Case and Ned knew that dance took up a lot of her time, though.

"Yeah, I'll be there," she said, wiping her plastic spoon clean. "Who are you playing today?"

"Mr. Branowski," Ned said, a big smile spreading across his face. His smudged eyeglasses seemed to flash with excitement.

"He must think you're pretty good," Ellie said, impressed. Mr. Branowski was an eighth-grade math teacher and the club's chess coach.

Ned shrugged, modest, and scooped up a big bite of pasta salad. He pushed the container toward Ellie and tilted his head.

"Oh, no thanks," she said. "It looks good, though," she added politely. It looked *fantastic*.

"It is," Ned agreed. "My foster mom loves to cook." Ned lived with Mrs. Juniper and a younger foster brother and sister. Mrs. Juniper had been taking care of Ned ever since his grandmother—who had raised him—had gotten sick.

"Is she—is she a *big* lady, Ned?"

"You mean is she fat?" Ned thought a moment. "No, just kind of squashy. You know, comfortable. It's nice for Franklin and the baby. They're still little. They like to cuddle."

"Oh, that's good." Ellie gathered the debris from her lunch and stuffed it back into the paper bag. She put the plastic spoon in her backpack. "Well, see you after school, I guess."

"Yeah, okay. Bye," Ned said. Now he was unwrapping his brownie.

How did boys stay so skinny? They must just be made that way, Ellie concluded, and she tossed away her trash.

When she stepped off the Eleventh Street bus that evening, it was already almost six o'clock. The way things were now, Tuesday was about her only normal day.

Ellie's arms ached as she lifted the heavy backpack over her shoulder one last time for the two-block walk home. She hoped her mom was in a good mood and that her father didn't fall asleep in front of the TV again.

Her father managed a small supermarket near

Queen Village. He had to get up very early in the morning, long before Ellie or her mother did. Maybe it was natural for him to be so tired by the time Ellie got home. But sometimes she felt as though his TV snoozing was more a way for him to hibernate for a while—like a bear in a cave—than a way for him to catch up on his rest.

The beauty salon her mom owned was down on South Street. Mrs. Lane often claimed that she worked as hard as she did mainly to pay for Ellie's ballet, but Ellie suspected her mother really liked being surrounded by other women intent on the same thing, on the pursuit of beauty. Ellie sometimes thought that might be the only thing left of her mother's early artistic yearnings. That and Ellie's dancing.

Ellie recalled how the fragrance of shampoo, nail polish, and coffee filled the air down at the salon. The whine of hair dryers, an undercurrent of music, and the soft sound of women's voices blended to create a soothing buzz. The beauty salon was like a cozy nest, Ellie thought—probably a lot cozier than home was for her mother.

And so her mother and father each had a hiding place.

Ellie's parents were a mystery to her. It was hard to imagine them ever being young and in love—but then everyone probably felt like that about their parents, she sometimes thought.

What had it been like for them, growing up in that

coal mining town? There hadn't been much money around, Ellie knew that much for sure. Her father had been the first in his family to attend college, but he had been forced to drop out when his own father had died.

And so he had started working in the grocery store to help support his mother. He had worked his way up to assistant manager by the time Ellie's mom started working there too, as a part-time checker.

Ellie had always loved the romantic tale when she was little. It had been told to her often—almost as a bedtime story—by her dad: Mr. Lane had fallen in love with the young woman who was always slipping off to the library during her brief lunch breaks. He had smiled as—for perhaps the fiftieth time—he watched her change the radio in the employees' lounge to the classical music station. This girl was *different*, he thought.

Ellie's mom had been orphaned by then, and was only nineteen when she married Ellie's father. Her husband was twenty-four. The following year his mother died, and Mr. and Mrs. Lane had moved to Philadelphia.

Ellie often studied old photographs of her parents, searching for pre-Ellie signs of unhappiness. Nothing: her father's boyish face was lean, not padded with an extra layer of flesh and disappointment the way it was now. His face was eager as it gazed at his young wife. Looking shy in one picture, she had held a blurry kitten to her chest. It was a lot easier to take care of a kitten than a baby, Ellie thought.

But having a baby a few years later had changed

things for the young Mr. and Mrs. Lane, Ellie guessed. She had overheard enough of her parents' quarrels to know a little of what had gone wrong for them: instead of attending evening concerts at the Curtis Institute of Music, for instance, or enjoying Sunday ballet matinées at the Academy of Music, as they loved doing, Mrs. Lane had started spending all her spare time and energy on the new baby.

Ellie always felt a little weird when she thought about that, as if she should apologize to someone—someone in the past. But how did you do that?

And rather than buying a yearly membership at the Philadelphia Museum of Art, as they had always done before, they'd begun spending all extra money on things for her, the baby—new clothes, a fancy stroller, and, later on, dance lessons.

I'm sorry, I'm sorry! Ellie wanted to tell someone.

Ellie knew that her father wanted her to have all these wonderful things when she was little, but she also saw now that at some point he must have begun to feel like a stranger in his own home, living with a couple of other strangers.

And then had come the awful day when Ellie was ten, and she had come home right after school one day, instead of going to dance. She'd had a bad sore throat. Her mom was still at work, but her father's jacket was on the dining room table. He was home early too.

Ellie had walked into her parents' room—the door was wide open—and then she had stopped, shocked.

Her father was packing a suitcase. It was on the bed, and his clothes were heaped around it. He was standing in the closet, holding some shirts on hangers, and he looked up and saw Ellie's reflection in the long mirror. Their eyes met.

Without a word he started to hang his clothes in the closet again. Ellie had turned, gone into her own room, and shut the door behind her.

Her father was there at the dinner table that night—silent, but there, at least. He and Ellie never spoke of that afternoon, and Ellie never told her mother about it, either. How could she have found the words? She tried to imagine saying, *Daddy has always wanted to leave because of me, but now he is staying because of me.* Would her mother thank her? Ellie didn't think so.

But it was as though her father had given up, that afternoon two years ago. It was almost like he had decided to sleepwalk his way through the rest of his life.

That left Mrs. Lane helpless, with no one to talk to or to argue with—no one but Ellie. In fact, the only thing her parents still seemed to have in common anymore *was* Ellie. She was like that sweet white stuff that holds the two cookie parts together, she thought, pausing to stare into the window of one of the antique shops that lined Pine Street. Hey, her mom even called her "sweetie" all the time, didn't she? When she wasn't complaining about how hard she had to work just to pay for Ellie's dance classes.

Ballet *was* expensive, Ellie had to admit: each class cost at least eight dollars, and she took four classes a week, with a few weeks off each summer. Once, she had figured it out on her calculator. She had been surprised to see that her classes cost over fifteen hundred dollars a year. Even if her family got some sort of discount, it was a lot of money.

And then there were the pointe shoes. Even with the fifteen-percent discount the dance store gave to advanced students, that came to a couple of hundred dollars a year. Add another hundred for regular ballet slippers and *another* hundred, at least, for tights and so on, and you came up with almost two thousand dollars a year, just for ballet.

If a person was getting paid seven dollars an hour, she would have to work almost three hundred hours to make that much money!

Maybe she *should* try out for the company, Ellie thought, unlocking the apartment house's big front door. At least then most of her classes would be free, and her mom might stop complaining about how hard she worked. *Or maybe I should just quit dance completely,* she thought.

And then what, she asked herself sarcastically as she climbed the stairs to her apartment. Would the Lanes live happily ever after?

No, being the frosting in the family didn't only mean holding the two cookie parts together, it also meant keeping them apart. And sometimes that seemed to be a part of her job description too.

My mom says a girl's neck should be like a stem holding up a beautiful flower, and Ms. Hawkins says a dancer's neck should be a strong slender column. Mine just looks disgusting, scrawny like a chicken's. I look like one of those bobble-head dolls, thanks to my neck. Can you do sit-ups for your neck? I know, I'll start rubbing lotion on the skin to keep it from getting all wrinkly. I can at least have a smooth chicken neck.

—To be continued.

3
Ellie's Neck

"And one, and two, and . . ." Ms. Hawkins tapped the cane on the studio floor in time with Mrs. Fiori's music. Ellie held the barre as lightly as she could with one hand and made the small circles called "rondes de jambe en terre"—which sounded like *rondajom-on-tare* and was French for "circles of the leg on the ground"—with her opposite foot. Friday class had begun.

"And turn," Ms. Hawkins said. The girls in Level Six turned to hold the barre with their opposite hands; each step was done for both sides of the body.

All the ballet terms were in French. Sure, it had

seemed strange at first, but Ellie had soon gotten used to it—five-year-olds can get used to just about anything. To French, to ballet positions, to quarrels behind closed doors.

Ellie remembered reading that ballet had started in the French courts more than two hundred years ago, and all over the world traditional French terms for the steps were still being used. Classically trained dancers could take class anywhere and understand what was going on. She liked being part of this, Ellie often thought. Sometimes she felt that ballet class was her real family; she could count on *it* never to change, at least.

Class always started at the barre, then moved to the middle of the room, then ended with the most strenuous exercise, grande allegro—the big jumps. Each class lasted ninety minutes. Dancers had to warm up with stretches first, so Ellie always allowed two and a half hours for each class. And that didn't count either getting to class or going home—add another hour for that.

"Leticia Elena, keep that neck long," Ms. Hawkins said to Ellie. "Don't hunch up like a warthog."

Ellie lifted her head up as high as she could without pointing her chin toward the ceiling. She could feel herself become a little taller, and looked straight ahead at her reflection—mirrors lined the room on all four sides—to see if she appeared any taller. Instead, though, she caught Dawn Upjohn's reflection, and she saw the smirk that was on Dawn's face.

Dawn had it all wrong, Ellie thought, biting her lip.

It was like she thought anything bad that happened to someone else worked out to something good for her.

This new phase of their relationship had started a few months ago. Before then—she admitted it—Ellie had competed with Dawn informally and secretly in ballet class. Could she do one more pirouette than Dawn? Could she get one less correction in class? Ellie was pretty sure Dawn was doing the same thing with her. Or she had been, before the temper tantrums had started.

But after all, hadn't the two of them been thrown into competition for years? They had never gone to the same schools, but since their mothers were friends, each had always been aware of what the other was up to. Ellie had heard, "Viv says Dawnie got a B in science, but an A in everything else." "Viv says Dawnie hasn't missed a day of school all year." So she had long thought of Dawn as a parent's idea of the perfect kid.

Had Dawn heard similar things about her, Ellie, as the years went by?

But while Dawn had always been a little moody, she had started really losing it a while back. She had fallen apart three times recently in the studio dressing room, once kicking a locker so hard that she had injured her foot. Naturally, she was sure it was broken, but it wasn't. Dawn did have to miss dance for two weeks, though.

And while in the past she had often been sarcastic

to others, Dawn was now so openly critical of everyone that many of the girls in Level Six had started
avoiding her.

Even with all these problems, Dawn rarely missed
class. But lately there were times when she never said
a word to anyone. Twice, she had run out of the room
in tears.

Ellie sighed, tired of the still-smirking Dawn and her
problems.

"Dawn," Ms. Hawkins said, "your arm is drooping,
and so is that wrist. No spaghetti hands, please." Dawn
stopped smiling. Her eyes flew to the mirror once
more, as though its shiny surface were magnetized.
Ellie stopped watching Dawn and started thinking
instead of the long evening ahead. She sighed again . . .

That morning, her mom had said, "Oh, Ellie, I forgot
to tell you—Viv Upjohn called last night. Dawnie has
an appointment this evening down the street from
here, and Viv asked if she could pick her up at our
house tonight."

"What? Why here?"

"Because we're so much closer to the appointment
than they are, sweetie," her mother explained patiently. "Dawnie can have dinner with us, then Viv will
come get her."

"But I don't want Dawn coming over here," Ellie
said. Seeing her at ballet four times a week was plenty.

30

"Oh, Ellie, don't be ridiculous—you two girls have known each other for ages. You have so much in common! Anyway, it's all settled. You'll come home on the bus together."

"Mom, please don't make plans like this for me, ever again."

"I didn't do it for you, Ellie. I did it for Viv."

"Well, just don't, okay?"

Her mother had stared at her, perplexed. "Ellie, I don't know what's gotten into you lately."

Maybe she had started having a mind of her own, that was all, Ellie thought angrily. Why should she have to go around feeling guilty for the rest of her life just because her parents were miserable?

"Would you like to come over to my house for dinner this Sunday?" Bella asked Ellie shyly after class. "My mother says she hopes you can. We could pick you up and everything." The Amorys lived in a beautiful old house in the Society Hill area. Ellie stopped brushing her hair, now free from its hated but required bun, and looked at Bella curiously. The two girls had never seen each other outside of class. "There's something I wanted to talk to you about," Bella confided.

"Well, sure, I guess I can come," Ellie said, intrigued. "I mean, I have to check with my mom, but she'll probably say yes."

In fact, Ellie knew her mother would be thrilled. Even though she sort of made fun of Bella, Mrs. Lane seemed to have become an expert on the

Amorys; she knew about their social activities, their money, and so on. Sometimes she pointed out Mrs. Amory's picture in the *Philadelphia Inquirer*, the city's biggest newspaper, when there had been some big fund-raising party.

"I could call you tonight and check," Bella said, "or you could call me."

"Why don't you just call each other and get it over with?" a cool voice suggested. Dawn was back from the bathroom. "I hope I'm not interrupting anything," she added sarcastically.

Ellie stuffed her hairbrush back into her dance bag and got to her feet, ignoring Dawn. "I'll call you tonight," she told Bella.

"Before nine, okay?" Bella said, blushing. "Daddy doesn't like calls coming into the house after that."

"Okay," Ellie said.

"Ellie, come on," Dawn said. "We'll miss the dumb bus."

"Dawn's supposed to come home with me tonight," Ellie explained to Bella.

"It wasn't *my* brilliant idea," Dawn said angrily, straightening her sweater. "You don't have to tell the world."

"I wasn't. I—"

"Oh, come *on*," Dawn said, disgusted. "Let's get this over with."

The two girls were silent during the short crosstown bus trip home. Dawn sat, Ellie stood. Why was Dawn blaming her for all this? Did she think Ellie wanted her to come over and play Barbies or something?

"This is it, isn't it?" Dawn was saying. "Ellie, wake up! Isn't this your stop?"

"What? Oh, yeah—off, please," she said, and they stepped off the crowded bus onto a nearly empty sidewalk.

"How far from here? I forget," Dawn said, staring down Pine Street.

"Only a couple of blocks," Ellie said. She shifted her dance bag and heavy backpack and started walking. "Why? What time is your appointment, anyway?"

Dawn blushed as she hurried to catch up. "What appointment?"

"I thought that's what your mom told my mom, that you had some appointment," Ellie said, confused.

"Well, it's not that big a deal, okay?" Dawn said, stumbling a little on the cracked pavement. "You don't have to make such a *thing* out of it. And it's not like I asked to come over to your house to eat. Anyway, I'm not even hungry."

"Well, that's good. It'll be something vegetarian, probably. My mom has been on this low-fat kick lately."

"It's probably healthier than what you'll get at Arabella's house, anyway," Dawn said, looking slyly at Ellie.

"I don't care," Ellie said with a shrug. "A change will be nice."

Dawn laughed. "Right. You can stuff yourself with caviar, and roast beef with gravy, and some kind of gloppy potatoes, and chocolate cake. Dinner at the Amorys'!"

"I don't think rich people really eat like that," Ellie said, "but whatever."

"That's right, *what*-ever," Dawn said. "And then you and darling Arabella can feed each other candies from a silver plate."

"She's not that fat, Dawn. Maybe ten pounds. And I'm sorry if my social life bothers you," Ellie said as they climbed the stairs to her apartment.

"I wouldn't touch your *so-called* social life with a ten-foot pole," Dawn hissed.

The door swung open, and Mrs. Lane stood silhouetted in the light. "Girls!" she exclaimed. "I was starting to get worried, and the eggplant is getting cold."

"Eggplant! My favorite!" Dawn said, giving Ellie a little poke between her shoulder blades. Her voice was sweet, though.

"I'm glad, Dawnie," Mrs. Lane said. "Oh, it's so nice to see you two kids together again."

In spite of her claim that eggplant was her favorite dish, Dawn barely touched dinner. Or rather, Ellie realized, she ate half—of everything. She ate half of the broiled eggplant, half of her salad, half a whole-wheat roll, and half an apple for dessert. Dawn's dinner plate looked as if a surgeon had bisected everything on it.

"You didn't eat much, dear," Mrs. Lane said to

Dawn, "but I guess you just weren't very hungry. I wish I could say the same," she added, looking down comically at the lower half of her body.

"Dinner was good, Mom," Ellie said, trying to excuse her own empty plate. She got up and carried some dishes into the kitchen. She looked up at the old electric wall clock: it was seven-thirty. Pretty soon Mrs. Upjohn would pick up Dawn for her appointment.

Ellie expected Dawn to follow her into the kitchen and help her wash the dishes. Instead, she heard the murmur of voices in the dining room. *Great,* she thought bitterly. Finally her mom had a kid she could talk to—only it was Dawn. She took her time with the glasses, plates, and silverware, imagining their conversation:

Oh, Dawnie, I just don't know what to do about Ellie. She's been so uncooperative lately.

Dawn might shake her head. *I know what you mean. She's a little like that in dance, too.*

Her mother would be horrified. *You mean she's having trouble in ballet?*

Oh, her technique's okay, Dawn would reassure her, pretending to be fair. *It's Ellie's attitude that's the problem. And that's bound to backfire on her—eventually.*

You mean at the company audition, Mrs. Lane would say, her voice low.

I'm afraid so, Dawn would say, finishing half her glass of water.

▶

Ellie shoved the pan into hot, sudsy water and scrubbed hard at the little burnt circles the eggplant had made while it had sizzled. Her father would have excused himself from the table by now—unless he had fallen for Dawn too! What if he had?

▶

What about at school? he might be saying, suddenly tired of being silent. *She's doing a good job at school, anyway. She's in those accelerated programs, after all.*

Well, Mr. Lane, Dawn would reply, *I hope so. But I go to St. Catherine's, you know, so I can't say for sure.*

I'm worried about that after-school chess club, Mrs. Lane might confide, as if she were talking to her friend Vivian instead of to Dawn. *Couldn't that be just another example of her lack of commitment to ballet?*

Oh, I don't know, her father might say, trying to defend Ellie—and to disagree with his wife in a safe way. *Ellie has made some pretty good friends in that club.*

If you say so, her mother would answer with a snort. *But it's hurting her dance—definitely.*

My *mother's very careful about who I hang out with after school,* Dawn would say. *But then she's pretty strict, I guess.*

Well, it certainly has paid off, Dawnie, Ellie's mother would say.

▶

Ellie crammed the roasting pan into the cupboard just

as the doorbell rang. Great timing, she thought, wiping her wrinkly fingers dry. Now she wouldn't have to listen to the Magnificent Dawn, at least—just to her own parents, united at last, raving about the perfect girl.

She pushed open the swinging door into the dining room; a jumble of napkins and a scattering of crumbs still littered the table's surface. She heard voices from the living room and reluctantly entered.

"Thanks, Mrs. Lane," Dawn was saying. She looked a little shaky, a little pale.

"You're welcome, Dawnie. Anytime," Ellie's mother said, her voice bright. There was no sign of Ellie's dad. "It was a pleasure, Viv," her mom continued. "I mean it. Anytime."

"Ellie," Mrs. Upjohn said, her red, lipsticked mouth stretching into a wide grin. "How pretty you look, dear."

Especially after doing all those dishes, Ellie thought, furious. Her face was red, she was sweating, and there was water all over her blouse. "Thanks," she said.

Dawn smoothed her perfect hair back with one hand. "Sorry I couldn't help, Ellie," she said, her voice sweet.

"Oh, that's okay," Mrs. Lane said. "Ellie's used to washing up," she added, turning back to Dawn's mother, "but it's not every day we get to have Dawn over."

"Well, we'll just see if we can't get these two young ladies together more often," Mrs. Upjohn said. "It would be just like the good old days," she added. Her voice sounded a little sad, though.

⊳

"Thanks for cleaning up, sweetie," her mother said a little while later. She shook the napkin crumbs onto the table and then started to wipe its surface clean with a damp paper towel.

"No biggie," Ellie said. "But, Mom?"

"What, Ellie?" her mother said.

"I wouldn't believe everything she says. Dawn, I mean."

Her mother looked puzzled. "Ellie, what on earth are you talking about?"

"I'm just saying Dawn and I aren't really such great friends. We never were, actually. And she would probably say anything to make me look bad, even in my own house. Oh, it's hard to explain," she added, turning away.

"Young lady, I think your imagination is running away with you," her mother said, holding the damp crumbs in her upturned hand. She looked as though she was about to start juggling them.

"Well, I only wanted to warn you," Ellie said.

"Ellie, Dawn Upjohn and I sat here in complete and utter silence after you cleared the table. Your father excused himself to go take a nap, big surprise, and so then I thought maybe we could have a nice little talk. I hoped so, anyway—Dawnie was such a sweet little girl, Ellie. The two of you together, playing!"

"That was a long time ago, Mom."

"Not to me. Anyway, I hoped I could get her talking about—about dance, maybe. Some nice, safe topic. But then she excused herself, too," her mother said.

Ellie made a noise that sounded like a snort. "So

Dawn excuses herself from helping with the dishes, and she excuses herself from talking with you. What was she doing all that time, anyway?"

Her mother had a funny look on her face. "Well, according to your father, who happened to be in the next room, she was in the bathroom—crying."

"*What?*" Ellie said, astonished. "But why?"

"Because she's seriously depressed, honey. That's what Viv says, anyhow. She's worried sick over it." Her mother shook her head.

"What do you mean, she's depressed?" Ellie asked, frowning. "She doesn't look sad to me. Just mad, most of the time. And she's always thinking she's sick or something. She's probably faking, Mom."

"Well, she's not faking the depression, Ellie," her mother said, "and Viv is trying to do something about it. She's been taking Dawnie in for professional help. That's what this appointment tonight was all about."

"But—but Dawn has always been kind of a pain," Ellie sputtered. "And she doesn't have anything to be depressed about."

"We don't know that. But sometimes it just happens anyway, from what I read," Mrs. Lane said with a sigh. "I guess it's been building up for a while, but Viv says things really changed for the worse about three months ago. She says Dawnie started shutting herself in her room then, and refusing to do things with the family. Viv is really worried about her, Ellie."

"Huh. If you say so," Ellie said.

But she didn't know *what* to think.

Middle school is really all about hair, and I can prove it. If you are having a bad hair day, you might as well stay home. The world will turn on you. Nothing will go right—classes, tests, nothing. Even lunch. But if your hair is looking good, you have a chance. Luckily, my hair is just about my best feature. And that fact is probably the main reason I'm doing okay at school. Advance self-improvement: Keep it looking good. Shampoo at least every other day, always use conditioner, use a comb for tangles, use a brush for shine.

—To be continued.

4 Ellie's Hair

"That's not what you're going to wear, is it?" her mother asked late that Sunday afternoon. Dr. Amory was picking Ellie up at five, in only half an hour.

"Bella *said* it was casual," Ellie replied, trying not to look at herself in the mirror while her mother was still in the room. Why give her the satisfaction? "Their Sunday dinners always are."

"Well, casual's one thing, but . . ." Mrs. Lane's worried voice trailed off, and the room was silent for a moment.

"Jeans and a sweater is casual, Mom," Ellie said. "There are no holes, and everything's clean—including my hair, you'll be glad to hear." Her mom never had to remind Ellie about washing her hair, but she always did anyway.

"Your hair looks nice, darling," her mother said, sounding as though she was eager to compliment her daughter on *something*.

It was true, though. Ellie's hair was a medium brown, which sounded ordinary. But it never looked boring; it was shiny and smooth, even when she was a bunhead. When she wore her hair down, which was all the time she wasn't dancing, its heaviness—which was emphasized by a straight cut kept perfect at her mom's beauty salon—made it her strongest point, Ellie secretly felt. Her eyes weren't too bad either.

Sometimes Ellie looked at herself in the mirror and tried to figure out why she looked the way she did. Where did a person's looks come from?

Her hair? It looked like her mother's, when her mom had been a little girl. Now, her mom's hair was permed and frosted; it was hard to tell *what* color it was anymore. Ellie promised herself she would never do that to her own hair.

Her green eyes? They were like her father's, though the gold flecks were more like her grandma's. Her oval face with its pointed chin was definitely her grandma's. The dimple came from her mom, probably.

Ellie's long legs came from her dad. Probably her shoulders did too, she thought gloomily. Her shoulders were too wide.

She wondered sometimes if any part of the way she looked was just hers. Her skin maybe; she always tried to keep it clean. Perhaps her figure was hers too. She was careful about what she ate—most of the time, anyway, and with her mother's nagging. Anyway, her posture was definitely hers. Well, hers and Ms. Hawkins's.

Ellie had finally decided that maybe you were born a certain way, but after that, what you did with it was up to you—more and more so every year. She hoped so, anyway. Ellie grimaced guiltily as she pictured her mother's bulges and her father's tired slump. Someday she would be a person separate from her parents and all their problems!

"Ellie?" her mother was saying. "Are you listening to me?"

"Sorry," Ellie said. "What?"

"Sweetie, I was saying that sweater's okay, but if I can't persuade you to change your pants, won't you at least change your shoes? You have those nice new ones."

"My sneakers are fine, Mom," Ellie said.

Her mother sighed, then changed the subject. "Now don't go eating everything in sight when you're there," she said, "but be sure at least to taste everything at least once."

"Okay," Ellie said. "I can always spit it out on the tablecloth if I don't like it."

"Ellie, for heaven's sake!"

"Look, give me a break," Ellie said, her patience gone. "It's just a meal, Mom. It's only food. You're always making fun of Bella—what do you care whether I behave like a yahoo at her house or not?"

"Ellie, I don't make fun of Arabella Amory. That's not fair. And I *do* care what others think of you—I admit it! I'm your mother, after all."

"What does that have to do with anything, Mom?"

"Plenty."

"But I'm almost thirteen! The way I dress isn't any reflection on *you*."

"Yes it is, and the way you behave is, too."

Ellie narrowed her eyes and tried to control her temper. "What about the way I dance, Mom?" she blurted out. "Is that *you* too? And—and what about the way you and Daddy act around each other? Is that supposed to be all my fault?"

Ellie's mother looked astonished. She opened her mouth to speak, but then the doorbell rang. Bella was at the door, Dr. Amory was waiting double-parked on Pine Street, and it was time to go.

The Amorys lived on Delancey Street, in the Society Hill section of Philadelphia. Their house wasn't all that far from Mr. Lane's market. Ellie wondered if Mrs. Amory ever shopped there—but she couldn't picture it.

Ellie used to think that Society Hill was named for all the rich people who lived there, but she knew now that—like many areas of Philadelphia—the district was a social patchwork. She also knew that "Society" didn't mean snobs, in this case. It wasn't short for the

Society of Friends, either, which was another way of saying Quaker, although Quakers had played an important part in the city's history. No, the Society Hill section had been named for the trading society that had been powerful in the area more than three hundred years ago.

There was really nothing to be nervous about, Ellie knew, but as she climbed into the waiting car, she felt as though she were stepping into a submarine to visit some foreign environment—a happy family, maybe. Oh, why had she said those things to her mom?

"Ellie?" Bella was saying. "This is my dad."

"Hi, Ellie," the man in the driver's seat said, turning awkwardly around.

"How do you do, Dr. Amory," Ellie said. She had been coached by her mother. Bella's father didn't look like Ellie's idea of a doctor, though; he looked as though he had been out hiking, or something.

"Heard a lot about you, from Bella. Glad you could come," he said, his voice cheerful.

"Oh, thanks," Ellie said, but Bella's father had turned his concentration back to driving.

"It's only chili for dinner tonight. I hope that's okay," Bella said softly.

"I love chili," Ellie said.

"My mom makes it with chicken—it's good. She made some corn bread, too, and a salad."

Ellie's stomach gurgled, and she hoped no one could hear it. Mrs. Amory cooked dinner, she thought, surprised. She had imagined that the tall blond woman she'd seen watching class occasionally—the woman whose hair was never mussed, whose clothes were always perfect—would have servants to take care of such things. Ellie felt both relieved and disappointed.

"We got lucky—there's a parking spot," Dr. Amory said, pulling up in front of a rosy brick house with black shutters and a fancy black iron fence in front. This part of the city was so old that very few houses had driveways. Dr. Amory probably drove his car each night to a nearby parking garage, Ellie decided.

The rooms inside the big house were mostly hidden from view by sheer gathered curtains. Ellie waited as Bella's father fumbled with his key, and she suddenly wished she had worn the new shoes instead of her sneakers. Well, she would have, if her mother hadn't come barging in! What would Mrs. Amory think?

"Ellie! We're so glad you could come," Bella's mother said, swinging open the big front door. She gave her husband a little kiss on his cheek. "Ready in ten minutes, Peter," she said. "And your beeper went off while you were out."

"Oh, no, I forgot it again," he said, patting at his waist.

"Don't worry, you always have Bella and me to look out for you," Mrs. Amory said playfully, winking at Ellie. "Listen, darling," she said to her husband, "why don't you go call the exchange? The girls can wash up and then help me set the table. They'll have plenty of time to visit after supper."

Ellie sneaked curious looks around her as she and Bella carried plates to the dining room. Instead of everything being either all very old or all entirely new, as she had imagined, the Amorys' rooms were a mixture of old and new furniture, old and new lamps. The pictures all looked old, though. Everything was very clean, and there was practically no mess, Ellie noticed, thinking of her own cluttered home.

She felt a sudden unexpected pang of sympathy for her mother, who was always trying to keep everything in the Lanes' apartment just so. Maybe this was what she had been aiming for. Margot Fonteyn could have moved right in.

To Ellie's surprise, dinner was fun. They served themselves from bright ceramic bowls set out on a side table, and they talked and laughed throughout the meal. Dr. Amory liked to joke, and he and his wife even looked as if they were flirting at times. That would be so weird, Ellie thought, trying to imagine her own parents doing the same.

"Bella, elbows," Mrs. Amory said once.

Once was all it took. Bella removed her offending elbow from the table and straightened her spine before her mother could correct her posture. Ellie sat up straighter too. "I've seen you in class, dear," Mrs. Amory said, beaming a bright smile at her. "You're very good."

"Thank you," Ellie said, embarrassed.

"You must be terrific," Dr. Amory observed. "My wife doesn't hand out compliments lightly."

Ellie looked at him, unsure of how to react. Was he complaining about Mrs. Amory?

"Is there any more chili?" Bella asked.

"I think you've had enough, darling," her mother said gently.

"But I'm still hungry," Bella objected.

"There's some left," her father said, lifting the lid and peering into the bowl.

"Then help yourself," Mrs. Amory said smoothly, smiling at Ellie. "More salad, Bella? Ellie?"

When her mom wasn't looking, Bella made a face at Ellie.

Boy, Ellie thought. Her own mom would probably have dragged the bathroom scales into the dining room by now to make her point.

"We'll go out for dessert if you girls are hungry later," Dr. Amory said, as if reassuring his daughter and her friend. "How does a frozen yogurt extravaganza sound?"

"Great," Ellie and Bella replied together. Mrs. Amory rolled her eyes.

Dr. Amory laughed. "Okay. You kids go on upstairs for a while—we'll leave here at eight-thirty. I'll take care of the dishes."

"Thanks, Daddy," Bella said, giving him a hug.

As the two girls climbed the stairs, Ellie slid her hand along the silky wood banister. "I think it's so great that your dad does the dishes," she said.

"Well, they both work," Bella answered with a shrug.

"I didn't know your mother had a job," Ellie said. "I mean, she comes to watch ballet class and everything."

"She only watches class when she can. I wish she *wouldn't*." Bella was bitter. "Sometimes it feels like she's taking over my life!"

"Yeah, I know what you mean," Ellie said, a little

surprised that Bella felt that way too. Mrs. Amory seemed so nice, even when she was saying all her mom stuff. Nice compared to Ellie's mother, anyway. Bella didn't know how lucky she was!

Ellie looked around Bella's bedroom. It was big— it even had a fireplace. And her bed, at least, matched Ellie's fantasies: a lacy canopy arched over it. Ellie imagined waking up in such a bed. Someone, a kindly old housekeeper maybe, would have lit a fire in the fireplace, and . . .

"So listen," Bella was saying, her voice serious. "You've got to help me. That's what I wanted to talk to you about."

Ellie pulled herself away from her daydream. "Why, what's wrong?" she asked, kicking off her sneakers and sitting cross-legged on Bella's big bed.

"I start with that coach tomorrow, after school. You know, getting ready for the audition."

"So you'll have to go to the coach *and* take class?"

Bella nodded. "It's pointe class on Monday. You know we can't miss pointe."

"Oh, yeah," Ellie said. "Well, but what can you do?"

"That's what you've got to help me figure out. I've been thinking like crazy," Bella said.

"What have you come up with so far?"

"Well, I thought about getting sick the day of the audition. But that would never work—my dad's a doctor. You can't fake anything with him."

"That's too bad. What about an injury? Faking it, I mean, not jumping in front of a bus or anything."

"No, they'd just rush me over to Daddy's hospital for x-rays and stuff. Maybe I could arrange a minor injury, though . . ."

"Bella, you—"

"Oh, not where I break my leg, necessarily. Nothing too drastic. But maybe a twisted ankle? I could always fall down a couple of stairs."

"But twisted ankles *hurt*. You're talking about bruises and swelling. You can't fake that," Ellie objected.

"I'm not talking about faking it."

"You'd really hurl yourself down the staircase?"

"Maybe at school," Bella said, nodding. "They'd freak, so many kids' parents are lawyers!"

Ellie laughed. "Well, let's see what else we can come up with first. How about . . . amnesia?"

"Or abduction," Bella said jokingly. "I could pretend to be kidnapped, and they'd be so relieved to get me back without paying any ransom, they'd forget all about the audition."

"Maybe *I* should try that one," Ellie said.

"Oh, Ellie—were you serious about not wanting to try out?"

"Well, maybe," Ellie admitted slowly. "I'd like to have a choice, at least. My mom acts like it's a given. That's what gets me."

"But you're so good!"

"Bella, if I get in the company, it means I'll be taking class Monday through Friday and then rehearsing all day Saturday. That pretty much rules out anything else, including a social life. Don't you think that should be *my* decision to make?"

"I don't think I'd care, if I could dance like you. My mom says you're a natural."

"Nobody was born doing ballet. We're both at the same level. It's not like you can't—"

"Oh, come on, you know what I mean. There's a difference, Ellie. I could never, ever join a professional company, for one thing."

"Would you want to?"

"I don't know. I'd like to be good enough to be able to," Bella admitted. "Like you. Like Dawn, too, for that matter."

"Do you think that's what Dawn wants to do?" Ellie asked. "She keeps saying how terrible she thinks she is, lately."

"You know her better than I do," Bella said, shrugging. "Does she want to keep on dancing? She seems pretty serious to me."

Ellie thought of telling Bella about the dinner Friday night, and about Dawn's problem, but her mom had told her to keep it confidential. "Well," she said instead, "I know what I could do to get out of the audition. Maybe I *will* do it, as a matter of fact."

"What?"

"Oh, maybe I shouldn't tell you. It's pretty radical," Ellie teased.

"*Ellie* . . ."

"Okay," Ellie finally said. "What's the worst thing a bunhead could ever do?"

"I don't know, what?" Bella asked.

"Cut off her . . ."

"Her what?" Bella asked, looking confused.

"Her bun!" Ellie exclaimed. Bella looked as though she couldn't believe what Ellie had said. "Her hair, that's right," Ellie said, nodding. "Just hack the old ballerina bun right off. Save it for Halloween, maybe. Put it on a plate with some Snickers bars and scare the little kids."

"But what good—"

"It's simple, really," Ellie explained. "You know how you have to wear your hair up once you get past a certain level in dance?" This rule was a firm tradition in the Philadelphia Dance Theater; female ballet dancers couldn't have short hair, because that wasn't traditional. They couldn't have medium-length hair, because it would get in their eyes during turns. No, girl dancers had to wear their hair up in a bun, with no bangs. This led to the "bunhead" nickname Ellie had overheard some male dancers use once; ever since, she hadn't been able to get the word out of her mind.

"You're right," Bella said slowly. "Ms. Hawkins would never make an exception to that company rule, no matter what."

"No," Ellie agreed. "It would be like spitting in the face of all that tradition. And can you imagine Ms. Hawkins spitting?"

Bella grinned at her and shook her head. "Ellie, you're positively brilliant."

"No, I'm not," Ellie said, laughing, "just twisted!"

"Okay, then, *twisted*," Bella agreed. "Now, listen— Daddy loves to treat, so order whatever you want to at the yogurt shop, okay?"

"If you insist," Ellie said.

Now, about my feet. Before we even get to how ugly they are, let me just announce that they're way too big. They look like clown feet, and pink satin toe shoes don't help. But underneath the shoes are bumps and lumps all the time, and blisters some of the time. Advance self-improvement: Start saving now for when I finally stop dancing. Maybe then I can get a foot transplant operation.

—To be continued.

5
Ellie's Feet

Each girl handled it differently: Michelle put moleskin pads between her toes before wrapping adhesive tape around her three smallest toes. Dawn wrapped each toe separately with paper tape after trying to add length to her middle toe with folded gauze. Bella simply wrapped wide paper tape around all her toes at once.

Ellie wrapped her big toes, covering the toenails, then put folded gauze between the next two toes. She finished by wrapping her littlest toes with adhesive tape. Paper tape slipped during class, she had found. At least pointe class was only once a week—so far—she thought with a sigh, as she snipped the heavy tape with the nail scissors she always carried. But maybe the calluses would build up when she had to take pointe more frequently.

Ellie's feet were almost finished. She stuffed the gauze, the tape, and the scissors into her dance bag. Then she tugged her tights down over her wrapped toes.

The previous November, about half of Level Six had been invited to take pointe on Mondays. "It's not something you can rush," Ms. Hawkins always said. "The body has to be mature enough. And I won't allow one of my girls to do it if she's not interested in going ahead with dance. It's too hard on the feet."

Still, each girl who had taken class long enough hoped desperately that Ms. Hawkins would decide that she was ready for pointe. They all longed to slip their feet into the satin toe shoes they had dreamed about when first starting ballet so long ago.

Ellie remembered years of watching older girls prepare for pointe class. She had stared in fascination at the girls' blotched and bumpy feet—so ugly, really, and so different from the rest of their bodies! Even Anne Marie Leone had weird-looking feet, and she looked like a model. But even when Ellie was looking at battered toes that had lost their nails, she'd longed for the day she too could dance on pointe.

"Remember when we first started pointe?" Ellie asked Bella when she had finally put away her supplies and resumed stretching.

Bella nodded, scrunching the paper tape around one of her feet. "We were so excited!" she said. "I was, anyway. You always looked like you knew what you were doing."

"Do you think this tape stuff really helps?" Ellie asked, looking at all the white-wrapped toes that surrounded her. The ballet waiting room looked like a hospital emergency room, she thought.

"A little. Maybe. But it's all part of the tradition, and anyway, you have to do *something*."

"Well, I know it helps me," Dawn said. "Maybe you should try the way I do it, Arabella, instead of just wrapping up your feet like a couple of big old burritos."

"She doesn't have to," Ellie said, glancing down at Dawn's tidily wrapped feet—which looked like puffy white origami, in her opinion. "Bella's middle toes aren't as short and stubby as yours, Dawn." That should keep her from picking on Bella, Ellie thought with only a small pang of guilt. They had tried to avoid one another since the night Dawn had eaten with the Lanes.

Dawn scowled as she tucked in the ends of her pale satin ribbons. Ms. Hawkins came out of her office and appeared to glide through the large, shabby room. She was like a small, tidy ship with black chiffon sails. "Ready, ladies?" she asked without looking back, as she disappeared into one of the three dance studios.

Ready as they'd ever be, Ellie thought.

◢

"Ellie, duck!" Ned cried out, but it was too late. A

crushed-up milk container sailed through the cafeteria and hit the back of her head with an almost cartoonlike *bonk*. She winced and touched her hair, hoping no milk had splattered on her.

"Hey, watch it!" Case yelled, but his voice almost disappeared in the noontime chaos. It was raining hard outside, and the population of Ben Franklin Middle School seemed to have doubled overnight.

"Are you okay?" Ned asked, concerned, as Case slowly took his seat again.

"I'm fine," Ellie said. Her voice was hardly shaky at all. "I mean, it's not like someone was aiming at me on purpose."

"They still hit you," Case said, and he bit into his apple with a ferocious snap.

"Where's the teacher who's supposed to be on duty, anyway?"

"Probably doing weapons searches," Ned said, trying to joke. He peered around the teeming room and shrugged.

Ellie tried to think of something to say to Case. Why was it so hard to talk to someone once you realized you really liked him?

"Hey, Ellie," Ned said, asking their usual lunchtime question, "did you finish your math?" Case had a different math teacher. He and Ellie had English together, though.

"Yeah, I finished," Ellie said, sneaking a look at Case. Oh, no—he was getting up to leave!

"I gotta go," Case said, wadding up his trash.

"See you," Ned said.

"Uh, Case?" Ellie asked, desperate for something to say. "Are you going to chess club this week?"

"I can't," Case said. "Why, are you?"

"No, I can't go either. I have dance," Ellie said. *Then why did you ask if he was going, dummy?* she raged at herself, but Case didn't seem to think she'd said anything unusual.

"Well, *I'm* going to chess," Ned said. "I'll definitely be there."

▲

"Ellie, have you given any thought to your birthday?" her mother asked at dinner that night. "Saturday will be here before you know it. If you're going to have a party—"

"I decided I don't want a party, Mom," Ellie interrupted. Better get it over with. "Not this year. But thanks anyway." She took a big bite of her turkey burger and pretended it was a real cheeseburger—although with all the things she'd piled onto it she couldn't tell the difference, she admitted to herself. Her dad looked as though he was enjoying his dinner, for once.

Mrs. Lane was visibly disappointed. "But, sweetie, this is such a special birthday. Thirteen years old! I thought maybe a boy-girl thing. Some dancing maybe, and a light meal to—"

"I know, Mom. But you don't understand. It just wouldn't work."

"We should let Ellie decide for herself," her father said. His voice sounded rusty, as though he hadn't used it in a long time.

56

Ellie's mother seemed to ignore him.

"But why, Ellie?" she said. "I've been looking forward to this for so long. I would have loved the chance to have a party when I turned thirteen," she added wistfully.

"This is my birthday, Mother. Look, when you were a kid, you went to a small school, right? Way out in the sticks."

"Well, it wasn't exactly Tibet," her mother said, sneaking a look at her husband and smiling a little. He smiled too.

"The point is, Ben Franklin's not like that," Ellie said. "The kids in sixth grade come from all these different schools, and then we have six periods a day, with different kids in each period. I mean, I have friends at school, but it's hard to really get to know anyone all that well. On top of that, the ones you *do* get to know don't know anyone else you know."

"Ellie, I don't know what on earth you're saying." Mrs. Lane glanced at her husband again.

"What about after-school activities?" Ellie's dad asked through a mouthful of salad.

"Thanks to dance, I don't *have* any after-school activities," Ellie said, "except for chess club—when I can go. And everyone in chess club is older, except for me and Case and Ned."

Mrs. Lane sighed.

"Mom, you barely even know them, and already you can't stand the thought of them," Ellie said, frustrated.

"Sweetie, it's not that I don't like Case and Ned. That's not being fair. I just think a chess party doesn't sound like the most fun thing in the world."

"Who said anything about a chess party?" Ellie asked. "You don't even want them coming over."

"Why, what's wrong with Case and Ned?" her father asked, sounding suspicious.

"Tell Daddy what you really don't like about them, Mom."

Her mother said, "Ellie, I—"

"I'd like to hear it," her father said.

"Mother found out that Case's dad is in prison," Ellie said flatly, hating the words even as she spoke them.

"For robbery," Mrs. Lane said.

"Well, it's not contagious," Ellie said, wanting to defend Case. "And Ned had to move into a foster home after his grandmother got sick and couldn't take care of him anymore. So *that's* what's wrong with *Ned*. See," she said to her father with exaggerated patience, "Mom likes the idea of me having friends, but she doesn't like the friends I actually pick."

"Oh, Ellie," her mother said.

Ellie's father cleared his throat. "Well, what do you like about Case and Ned, Ellie?" he asked.

"They're smart, and they're funny," Ellie said, sounding reluctant. Could she actually convince her parents? "We have fun together at school. And they don't complain, no matter how hard things get for them. Not that they're my boyfriends or anything."

"Ellie," her mother said, "I didn't mean to imply—"

"You choose everything else for me," Ellie interrupted heatedly. "Don't I even get to choose my own friends?"

"Ellie," her father said, "I think you might be acting a little unfair here."

"I don't know how we got off on this tangent, anyway," her mother said, looking helplessly up at the ceiling as though it might answer her. "I was merely talking about your birthday, Ellie. If you don't want a nice party, just—"

"I don't want a nice party or a lousy party," Ellie interrupted again, her voice wobbling. "I don't want to invite a bunch of boys I don't care about over to dance with a bunch of girls who don't even know each other, just to make you feel good, Mom. I don't want to make them eat—oh, disgusting turkey burgers and carrot sticks," she added, looking down at her plate. Wonderful, she thought, now she was going to cry. Or her mom was.

"Ellie, calm down," her father said. "What *would* you like to do to celebrate your birthday this year? Anything? Nothing?"

Was he serious? "Not dancing," Ellie said, sounding anxious, "and no big party."

"We could have a little party," her mother said. "Just a few—"

"Let's let Ellie say what she'd like," her husband interrupted gently, raising his hand like a traffic cop. "What would be your perfect birthday this year?"

Ellie looked at her mom, who nodded slowly. "I'm listening," she said.

"Well," Ellie said reluctantly, twining her feet around battered chair legs, "if you really mean it, I guess my ideal birthday would be for just a couple of friends—maybe three—to come over and eat. Pizza, or something. We could even send out for it," she said, sneaking a look at her mother.

"Pizza, how fun!" Mrs. Lane said, looking brave.

"And then we'd rent a couple of videos—ones that *we'd* choose," Ellie added hurriedly. "Nothing horrible, but they might be really dumb," she warned. "And then after that, we might have some birthday cake and ice cream, or maybe just go out for big old ice cream sundaes."

"Who would you like to invite?" her father asked. "If you could choose," he added, glancing at his wife before she could make any suggestions.

"Oh, I guess maybe Ned and Case," Ellie said casually, sneaking another look at her parents. "And I'd ask Bella. She doesn't know those guys, but we'd all have fun together, I think. It wouldn't be like this big boy-girl thing, though," she added. "It would just be . . . fun," she repeated.

"You'd invite Bella?" her mother asked, frowning.

"Why, what do you have against Bella, Mom?"

"Nothing. I—It's just that she probably goes to so *many* parties. Things come a little too easily for the Bellas of this world, if you ask me."

"That's not true," Ellie said. "You just don't know her."

"Well, what do you think?" Mr. Lane asked after a

silent moment, turning to his wife as if challenging her. "How does a pizza party sound?"

"It sounds okay," Ellie's mom said slowly, although she didn't really seem convinced. "But what about also inviting Dawn, Ellie? You and she were always—"

"We were always fighting behind your back, Mom," Ellie said flatly.

Mrs. Lane looked disappointed, but then her face brightened and she said, "Well, I could always make the pizza for your party. I found this low-fat recipe with broccoli, where you—"

"You can make low-fat broccoli pizza for *me*," Ellie's father announced. "We can eat it while we're staying out of Ellie's hair on Saturday night."

Whoa, Ellie thought. This was the most cheerful she had seen her dad act in ages!

Mrs. Lane blushed a little. "I guess—I guess one night of junk food wouldn't hurt you, Ellie," she said. "There would still be an entire week before the company audition. We'll get you back in shape. I just hope your face doesn't break out from all that grease."

"I could still dance, even with a bad complexion," Ellie said. *If I wanted to*, she added to herself.

"Well, it's settled, then," her mother said, straightening her knife. "Shall I pick up some party invitations? I saw these darling ones downtown the other day."

"No, Mom," Ellie said firmly. "Thanks anyway, though," she added in a softer tone. Hey, her mother was really trying. "I'll just invite them over the phone."

"Okay," her mother said, a little doubtfully. "If you're sure."

"I'm positive," Ellie said. She couldn't believe it, but she was actually starting to look forward to her birthday! "I'll do the dishes. You guys relax," she said.

"We'd *better* take it easy, while we have the chance," her dad joked. "But I'll help you clear, Ellie."

▲

"Thanks, Daddy," Ellie said to him in the kitchen. "For everything." Every so often, he really came through. He'd even made the ultimate sacrifice for her—health food pizza!

"No problem," her dad said. He stacked the dirty dishes next to the sink. "I'm glad you're going to have a party, Ellie. Your mother is right, turning thirteen is special."

Ellie started running the hot water. "Well, yeah," she finally agreed, "but not if you end up having the kind of party you hate."

"I think your mother would have liked to have *any* kind of party when she turned thirteen," Mr. Lane said, keeping his voice low. "It just wasn't in the cards, though."

"How come?" Ellie asked. Apart from the famous ballet story, her mother never talked much about her childhood.

"Well, let's just say it was partly money, and partly the people involved," her father said. "Maybe she'll tell you about it herself someday. But she always wanted things to be a little more pleasant for you. A *lot* more pleasant."

"Mmm," Ellie said, not meeting his eyes. She squirted detergent into the sink and watched the bubbles pile up. "You guys do everything for me, don't you?" she finally asked.

"What do you mean, Ellie?"

"Oh, you know," Ellie said. "Mom is always arranging my life. And you—well, I mean, you're *here*, aren't you?" Her voice sounded strangled as she said this.

Ellie's father reached over and turned off the water. "Ellie," he said, "I'm here because I want to be." His body seemed to grow tense as he spoke, as if he had suddenly found himself on a tightrope wire.

"But *why* do you want to be here?" Ellie asked.

"I like to finish what I start," he said simply. "I—I guess I decided that a deal's a deal. And a situation can always improve, if you work at it. I think maybe it's time for me to start trying a little harder." He cleared his throat.

"You were getting ready to leave that day," Ellie whispered. "You were packing, Daddy."

Ellie's father shifted from foot to foot as though willing himself not to run from the room. "I know I was, baby, but—well, maybe I came to my senses when I saw you standing there," he said. "And I'm grateful for that. Sneaking out would have been no solution." He glanced yearningly at the kitchen clock.

"But maybe you should have left! You're not happy here."

"Well, I know I haven't been the most cheerful guy

in the world lately," her father admitted, "but that's *my* problem. Running away wouldn't have been the answer."

"So you didn't stay just for me?" Ellie asked.

"No," her father answered, giving her shoulder a squeeze, "much as I love you, baby. I—I guess I stayed for *me*. I want to be married. I want to be part of a family, Ellie. And hey," he said, forcing a laugh, "you guys are it. I guess maybe I should be making that clearer—to *everyone*."

The thought of her dad wanting so much to be part of a family suddenly made Ellie blink back tears. First he'd lost his father when he was young, and then his mother had died . . .

"I'm sorry if it's been a little tense around here lately," Mr. Lane was saying, his voice gruff.

"That's okay," Ellie mumbled.

"Just—well, just try not to take things so personally, okay?" her father asked, a pleading look in his eyes. "Your mother and I are doing the best we can."

"I know you are," Ellie said.

Mr. Lane smiled a little upon hearing these words. "You mean it?" he asked.

"Sure," Ellie said, giving an embarrassed shrug. "Of course I do, Daddy."

Her father took a deep breath and then held out his arms, a question in his eye. Ellie wiped her damp hands on her sweatshirt and then—for the first time in a long time—they were hugging.

Ellie picked up the receiver and dialed. "Hey, Bella," she said, when her friend answered. She twisted the phone cord around one hand and looked over her shoulder, making sure she was alone in the darkened living room.

"Hi, Ellie. I can't talk very long—"

"I know, I just wanted to ask you if you wanted to come to this party on Saturday."

"You're giving a party?" Bella asked. She sounded amazed.

"It's my birthday," Ellie said, almost apologetic.

"Okay, sure! Who else is coming?"

"Well, that's the thing. I wanted to ask these two friends from school. Case and Ned."

"But—but those are boys, aren't they?" Bella sputtered, as if it wasn't obvious. "I don't even know them! And they don't know me."

"I know, I know," Ellie soothed her. "Don't panic, I haven't even called them yet."

"Oh," Bella said, clearly relieved. "Well, I don't know . . ."

"Look," Ellie said, taking a deep breath, "*you* go to an all-girls school, right?"

"Right," Bella admitted.

"And *I* have the most overprotective mother in the world, right?" Ellie continued.

"Well, right," Bella said. "But mine comes in second. A *close* second."

"And for whatever reason, a miracle happened," Ellie continued, "and my parents agreed to let me have this thing. And the way I figure it, this may be our one chance to actually participate in a boy-girl party, Bella."

"I didn't know you even wanted to," Bella said. "And I don't know those—"

"We're probably the only girls in Level Six who haven't been allowed to go to a party like this," Ellie cajoled her. "Maybe we should just get it over with. It'll be good for us! It almost doesn't matter what boys I invite," she added unconvincingly.

"Well, if you put it like that," Bella said, "it sounds almost like a science experiment." She giggled.

"I think we should do it," Ellie urged her.

"And it *is* your birthday," Bella said.

"Yeah. I think we should do it," Ellie repeated.

"*O*-kay," Bella finally said, slowly. "I'm pretty sure I can come."

"Good," Ellie said, and she sighed with relief. "Now, all I have to do is get up the nerve to call Ned— and Case." Case!

Here's a riddle: What's big, and round, and so totally flabby and out of shape that I can't even believe my eyes? Right—my future stomach. I have to start working on it right now. One hundred sit-ups a day, two hundred if I eat dessert. (Fruit doesn't count.) And for more advance self-improvement, no more chocolate— except on special occasions (right, like a day of the week that ends with Y).
     —*To be continued.*

6
Ellie's Stomach

It was May 18th, and Ellie Lane was thirteen years old.

She awoke early that morning, even though it was a Saturday. Lying in bed, Ellie thought back over her life so far. She couldn't remember much before age seven. It was like she really woke up then, she thought. Case Hill's little sister, Lily, had just turned seven; Ellie wondered if Lily was starting to wake up now too.

But if she came to life when she was seven, that meant she was really only six years old now. Ellie smiled. It felt more like she was a hundred years old sometimes! What would the *next* six years bring, and would they go by as slowly as the last years had?

In six more years she would be turning nineteen, Ellie thought, amazed. She would probably be in college by then—or she could even be dancing professionally. But she knew she wouldn't be living at home, anyway. She stretched comfortably, imagining a life away from the apartment on Pine Street.

"Happy birthday, baby!" her father said at breakfast. "Too bad you don't get the day off." Ellie had ballet class, and the audition was only one week away.

"Oh, I'd just sleep if I didn't have ballet," Ellie said. "Where's Mom?"

"She's getting ready for work," Mr. Lane said. Saturday was the busiest day of the week at the beauty salon. "But what would be wrong with you sleeping late?" Ellie's dad continued, smiling. "Teenagers are supposed to sleep a lot."

Her dad had said *teenagers!* That was her now, Ellie guessed, surprised and pleased.

"Hey, I got you something up the street," her dad said, his voice casual. He pushed a small gold box across the table toward Ellie's cereal bowl.

Ellie's stomach gave a little jump as she picked it up. *Up the street* could mean anything, she thought, although Pine Street was famous for its antiques—furniture, textiles, jewelry. "Thanks, Dad," she said. "Should I open it now, or wait?"

"Now," he said, grinning. "Later, all your rowdy

friends will be here scarfing down pizza and who knows what. You better do it while I have your attention."

Ellie tugged at the lavender ribbon that encircled the box. Inside, snowy tissue hid her gift. She lifted the tissue with a fingertip. "Oh, Daddy," she said.

A pair of antique earrings lay nestled in the box. They were very delicate: small round opals were surrounded by oval seed pearls, creating two small daisies. Ellie loved them on sight. And best of all—the earrings were for pierced ears!

Ellie had wanted to get her ears pierced since she was nine, but her mother had always said no. Well, she had said a lot more than that, but it all boiled down to no, which was weird, since she owned a beauty salon. One woman who worked there had a daughter who wore three earrings—in each ear! But Mrs. Lane had always said, "I want better for you, sweetie. You're a ballerina, and that's the most beautiful dancer there is. Ballerinas don't go covering themselves with trashy jewelry."

Finally, Ellie had given up trying to get permission. She would just get *everything* pierced when she moved away, she had thought, bitter.

But now . . . "Does Mom know?" she asked her father. Was this going to start more trouble?

"It was her suggestion," he said, surprisingly. "Something gave her the idea that maybe she was being a little extreme." Ellie tried to imagine this conversation, but she couldn't. "I got to pick out the earrings," her father continued. "She'll take you over to get the actual piercing done. I'd probably pass out cold. It won't be until next week, though," he warned, "and you'll have to wear simpler earrings at first. Then you can wear these. Do you really like them?"

"I really *love* them," Ellie said. She got up and gave him a kiss on his forehead. "Thanks, Dad."

"Well, thank your mother too. She's the one."

Ellie's mom gave her two presents just before she and Ellie left the apartment. "One's not much of a surprise," she said, apologizing in advance.

"I'll open that first, then," Ellie said, and she unwrapped the large box. Inside were extra-nice dance clothes: a pair of soft pink knitted leg warmers; a pair of loose-fitting nylon leg warmers, steel-gray; a black chiffon skirt, just like the one Anne Marie Leone wore during rehearsals; and two unitards, one black and one teal.

Since students always had to wear the required clothes in dance class—pale pink tights and shoes, black leotards—their one chance at variety was rehearsals. There would be lots of rehearsals if she became a member of the Philadelphia Dance Theater. Obviously, her mom was trying to tell her she had to audition. "Thanks, Mom," Ellie said, her voice neutral.

"I wouldn't expect you to throw out your baggy T-shirt collection or the ripped sweats, of course," her mother teased.

"No such luck."

"These will look terrific on you, though," her mother said. "Here, open the other gift now. You can return it if it doesn't fit, or something."

Like if she hated it, Ellie thought nervously. She opened the second present—and she loved it. "Oh, Mom!" she said, holding up the beautiful hand-knit sweater from Feathers, Ellie's favorite shop.

It had a gently rolled neckline and was made from the softest wool imaginable. It was all one color, a pale rose, but it combined several knitting stitches to create a sweater different from any Ellie had ever seen. "I thought maybe with a pair of black Levi's . . ." her mother suggested shyly.

"I'll wear it tonight," Ellie said, and she gave her mom a big hug—the first in ages. "Thanks," she added.

"Now, you better scoot," her mother said, flushed but pleased. "You know Ms. Hawkins won't let you take class if you come in late, even if it *is* your birthday."

"I know. And—and Mom?"

"Mmm?"

"Thanks for the earrings too. Daddy told me about that whole thing really being your idea."

"Well, I have to admit he got a kick out of picking them out. I'm glad you like them, sweetie. You know I've always said the last thing a classical dancer needs is two more holes in her head, but you seem determined to mutilate yourself. Now, scoot," her mother repeated.

It was almost time! Bella had arrived early, exactly as the two girls had planned. Case's neighbor was driving him and Ned over; the two boys would be arriving any minute. "What time did you say?" Bella asked.

"I told you, six-thirty," Ellie said.

"And you're sure they know *I'm* going to be here?"

Ellie nodded. "But remember," she said, "this is no big deal. We just have to get our first party over with, we don't have to get all nervous about it. And it's better than sitting around at home all night, or babysitting."

"Yeah," Bella agreed. "Um, Ellie?"

"What?"

"This is sort of hard to ask, but is either Case or Ned kind of like . . . your boyfriend? You never actually said."

Ellie blushed a little. "Jeez, Bella, you're as bad as my mom."

"Sorry, I just thought I better find out."

"Oh, that's okay," Ellie said, relenting. "I guess it's a fair question. But can you keep a secret?"

Bella nodded, her oval face solemn. Blond curls bounced. "You know I can."

"Well, it's kind of complicated. I'm better friends with Ned at school, and I think Case has this feeling that I really like Ned. Which I do, but as a friend."

"But it's really Case you like?" Bella asked, her voice low.

Now it was Ellie's turn to nod.

"Oh, Ellie, that's so romantic," Bella said.

"But complicated," Ellie repeated. "And Case doesn't know," she added.

"Well, *that's* romantic. Oh, I'm nervous! Do you have butterflies in your stomach too?"

"Butterflies? I have—"

The doorbell rang.

For the first two or three minutes of the party, Ellie was sorry she'd ever had the idea. Bella was silent, Case and Ned jostled each other and laughed loudly, and Ellie was talking too much, she realized. She even found herself wishing her parents would stick around and organize things after they'd greeted everyone.

But then the kids decided to order pizza. They sat on the sofa, heads bent solemnly over the battered take-out menu, and—after much discussion—phoned in their order: two extra-large pizzas, with everything except anchovies on them, to be delivered as soon as possible. "I think anchovies would be a big mistake," Ned said. They all agreed.

"Hey, why don't you open your presents?" Case suggested. Ellie opened Bella's card first. It pictured one of Degas's ballet paintings.

"That's pretty," Ned said, trying to get a closer look.

"Bella's a really good dancer," Ellie said, and Ned looked at Bella with new interest.

"I'm not as good as Ellie," Bella protested. She was blushing, but she looked pleased. "Open the present," she said, trying to change the subject.

"Oh—thanks, Bella!" Ellie exclaimed, holding up a big book of behind-the-scenes dance photographs.

"Open my present next," Ned instructed Ellie. "The card first." Ned's card was a cartoon of two genius scientists working out an equation. "That's us, in math class," he joked.

"Yeah, right," Ellie said, laughing. She unwrapped his gift, which was very heavy: it was a beautiful chessboard, made from squares of different kinds of polished wood. "Oh, Ned!" she said.

"I found it at Treasure Trove," he said. "That's Case's antique shop," he added, leaning toward Bella. "He got me a discount."

"I don't actually own the store," Case said modestly. "I just work there. Here, Ellie." He pushed his card and gift her way as if they weren't worth bothering with.

Case—famous at school for his cartooning—had made Ellie's birthday card. "Oh, it's Spotty!" Ellie said, laughing. Spotty was a cartoon character Case had invented; he held a bunch of balloons that spelled out *Happy Birthday, Ellie.* "Thanks, Case," Ellie said.

"Open the present now," he urged, his shyness gone.

Ellie started to undo the tape that held the wrapping paper together. "Just rip it off," Ned said with a grin.

"Okay," she said. When the colorful paper was in shreds, she carefully opened the white cardboard box. "Oh," she said.

Everyone craned forward to see: Case had made Ellie a complete cartoon-style chess set. He'd inked in the figures on both sides of heavy cardboard, cut them out with a mat knife, and then slid each one onto a slotted wooden base. One group of figures was dogs, and the other was cats—a cat king and queen, cat bishops and knights, each one funnier-looking than the last. "You did this yourself?" Bella asked, amazed.

"It came out great, Case," Ned said. "Look!" He held out a snooty-looking dog king, and Ellie and Bella laughed.

"I think it's incredible that you made this whole set," Ellie said, echoing Bella. "It's wonderful."

Ellie's mom poked her head into the room. "Hate to interrupt," she said, "but pizza's here."

"I'm stuffed," Case said, and he groaned.

"I can't believe we ate both pizzas," Bella said, sounding dazed.

"I can," Ned announced, businesslike. He peeled a puddle of cold, leftover cheese from the cardboard pizza carton and dropped it into his mouth.

"He's like this at school, too," Ellie observed to the group. She lowered her voice, sounding like a scientist on a TV documentary: "Ned eats, and eats, and eats some more—but he never, ever gets full."

"That's right," Ned said complacently.

"Well, *I'm* full," Bella said.

"You guys want to walk over to the video store?" Ellie asked.

"Does that involve actually moving?" Case asked, as if she had suggested they all fly around the block.

But they managed to get up, clatter down the stairs, and make their way to the corner video store. Since the sidewalks were narrow, Ellie ended up walking next to Case. Bella and Ned walked side by side too, behind them. "That's a pretty sweater," Case said. "You look good in pink."

"Thanks," Ellie answered, blushing a little. She was relieved it was dark out.

"How about this one?" Ned suggested when they had reached the store, holding up an empty video box. It showed a monster—the gooey kind—towering over a little girl.

"Perfect," Ellie declared. "Let's get another, too. That way if we hate one of them, we can switch."

They tumbled out of the video store and headed back to the Lanes' apartment. Somehow, Case ended up walking next to Ellie again, but behind Ned and Bella this time. Case swung the video bag by its string, and his free hand brushed once against Ellie's. His hand hesitated there, as if it had a mind all its own that had just about decided it was time to hold Ellie's hand. But by then they arrived at the front door of the apartment building. Ellie felt relieved and disappointed at the same time.

The four of them pounded back up the stairs. Mrs. Lane had made popcorn, and its fragrance filled the rooms. They piled all the sofa pillows onto the floor and flopped down on them. They started watching the scary video. It turned out to be so funny, though, that soon the four of them were gasping with laughter.

"Don't choke on your popcorn, Ned," Ellie said.

"Or we'll have to perform . . . space-alien surgery," Case said, hoisting an imaginary dagger high in the air.

"Without anesthetic," Bella added enthusiastically.

"I'm chewing, I'm chewing!" Ned protested feebly. "See?"

"But still he never, ever gets full," Ellie announced, the TV scientist once more.

After they'd seen most of the movie, Ellie's dad popped his head around the corner. "Psst, Ellie," he said. "Are you kids through watching that extremely wholesome flick?"

Ellie laughed and nodded. "Yeah, the best parts are over. And there's not really time to watch the other video."

"Then, here," her father said, handing her some money. "For ice cream. But you guys be back by ten-thirty, okay? That's when I said I'd take your friends home."

Ellie glanced down at the money in her hand. "Thanks, Daddy," she whispered. "We'll be back."

They each had a banana split.

"Oh, my stomach. I think I'm going to pop," Case said as they staggered back to the Lanes' apartment.

"Me too," Ned said.

"It's nothing that a few thousand sit-ups can't take care of," Ellie joked.

"Or a few days of fasting," Bella added.

"But it was worth it, wasn't it?" Ned said, grinning at Bella. "I mean, hot fudge!"

"If people everywhere ate hot fudge sauce at least once a week, the world would be a better place," Case intoned. "There would be peace, and harmony, and—"

"And liberty and pimples for all," Ned finished, laughing. "But it would be worth it," he repeated with a happy sigh.

In bed late that night, Ellie thought back over her birthday: the presents, the pizza, the video, the ice cream.

And then there was Case to think about—Case, who had finally held her hand on the way home from the ice cream store. It had only been for a few seconds, but Ellie had thought her heart might stop. She knew she would never forget it.

What a birthday.

And her parents had been pretty cool about everything, she had to admit. It had almost been like being part of a normal family. Now, if she could just get her mom off her back about the audition . . .

No, she thought, snuggling deep into her covers, worries could wait. It had been a great day.

In fact, she couldn't wait to talk it over with Bella tomorrow. That would be almost as much fun as the party itself!

Talk about bizarre! I guess my ears aren't any weirder than anyone else's. They just stick out more—when my hair is in a bun, anyway. When you stare at them for a long time, they look even funnier, like little pink head handles. Though I guess if you stare long enough, anything will start to look funny. Well, at least pretty soon my pink head handles will have decorations on them: my new earrings!

—To be continued.

7
Ellie's Ears

"Your earrings look great," Bella said to Ellie. Her voice was low. It was Wednesday, and Level Six would be starting in another ten minutes. Ellie neatly folded her new sweater and put it in her dance bag, being careful not to snag the wool when she zipped the bag shut. The two girls started to take turns pushing down on each other's extended feet; their theory was that this helped to increase flexibility.

"Thanks," Ellie said, pausing to touch her tender earlobes. "These are just temporary, though. You have to wear them until the piercing heals."

"Did it hurt much?" Bella asked.

"A little," Ellie admitted. She could still hear the *ka-CHUNK, ka-CHUNK* of the ear-piercing gun. "It sounded worse than it felt," she added.

"Well," Bella said with a sigh, "I guess you and I were about the last two girls in Philadelphia who didn't have *something* pierced. Now I'm the only one. Hey, maybe my mother will let me get my ears pierced, now that you've done it first."

Ellie laughed a little. "I doubt it. Why don't you start asking if you can get your nose pierced? Maybe then the ears won't seem like such a big deal. Or—I know! Start saying you want a tattoo. Tell her my mom's thinking about letting me get one."

"Yeah, right," Bella said. "Like she'd believe that." She sighed. "My mom really likes the way you look, I can tell."

"She likes the way *I* look?" Ellie asked, amazed. "Bella, you guys look just like each other! You're both blond, you're both pretty."

"There's one big difference. My mother is skinny, and she always has been," Bella said, making a funny face. "There's proof in all the old photo albums. She was perfect."

"She probably didn't *feel* perfect," Ellie pointed out.

"Hey, whose side are you on?" Bella asked, only half joking. Then she added, "Oh, my mom doesn't criticize me out loud, or anything. She just raises her eyebrows at me a lot and praises everyone else. Like *you*, Ellie."

"I'm sorry," Ellie said.

"It's not your fault," Bella reassured her. "Anyway, my mom probably thinks she's being all subtle and everything. But I'm a big disappointment to her, I can tell. Hey," she said, making an effort to change the subject, "did you hear?"

"No, what?" Ellie asked.

"Well, two things—one's about Dawn, and the other's about Anne Marie."

"Anne Marie Leone? What about her?"

"She's quitting dance after this week!" Bella announced. "And Dawn—"

"Wait a minute," Ellie said. "What do you mean, Anne Marie is quitting dance? She's just a junior in high school. There's a whole 'nother year she could be in the company."

Bella shrugged. "I'm just repeating what I heard. She's not even coming to the audition on Saturday." The yearly audition took the form of a regular company class. All those older kids watching—it was one of the things that made Ellie so nervous.

"But why?" Ellie asked. "Push harder," she added. Bella pressed Ellie's pointed toes toward the gray-carpeted floor.

"I heard maybe she was getting married," Bella whispered, leaning forward.

"Oh, come *on*," Ellie said.

Bella was offended. "Well, I don't know! Why ask me? I was only saying what I heard, that's all."

Ellie thought about this as the two girls switched places. She gripped Bella's feet and gently pressed down. "Am I doing it too hard?"

"No, it's okay," Bella said, grimacing a little. "I already stretched once this afternoon."

"Oh, yeah! How's the—the you-know-what going?" Ellie asked, remembering the ballet coach Mrs. Amory had hired.

"Wonderful," Bella said in her most sarcastic voice. "I have such *potential*," she mimicked. "Such potential to make a fool out of myself this Saturday, anyway," she added bitterly.

"So she's not helping?"

"Not enough. Maybe if we'd started when I was ten." Around them, girls were sliding slowly into splits. "We better finish up," Bella said. "Now, do you want to hear what everyone is saying about Dawn, or not?"

"I guess," Ellie said reluctantly. "I thought she was just sick or something," she added. Dawn hadn't been in pointe class on Monday.

"It's worse," Bella said softly. "She's seeing a psychologist!"

"Where'd you hear that?" Ellie asked.

"From Michelle," Bella said after looking cautiously around. Michelle was nowhere in sight just then. "Well, I heard her telling this other girl. Dawn is seeing this psychologist, and that's why she's not here. It must be serious, don't you think?"

Ellie sidestepped the question. "What's so bad about seeing a psychologist?" she asked. "That's not so terrible. And anyway, I don't see how that ties in with her not being here. That just doesn't make sense—Dawn could do both things, couldn't she?"

"Well, she *isn't* here," Bella pointed out. "That makes two days in a row she's missed—and right before the company audition, too. You don't think that's weird?"

"I guess it is," Ellie admitted.

"Why are you defending her, anyway?" Bella asked. "I thought you hated her."

"I don't *hate* her," Ellie said, picturing Dawn's pinched, unhappy face as she stood in the Lanes' apartment that Friday night. She felt kind of sorry for Dawn, she realized.

"Ladies," Ms. Hawkins's voice called out. "Mr. Jeffries will be teaching class for me today. And it's time, please—don't keep him and Mrs. Fiori waiting. You all have plenty left to learn, believe me."

Class was hard, but Ellie always liked it when they had other teachers. Even though the basic steps never changed, each teacher came up with different combinations.

"And one," Mr. Jeffries said at the end of class, "and two." The girls in Level Six made their deep curtsies toward Mrs. Fiori's corner. She beamed a broad smile back at them and closed up her sheet music. The girls clapped politely as they made their murmuring way to the door. Ellie's ears caught the word "Dawn" once or twice, but she couldn't hear details of what anyone was saying. There was too much noise.

In the waiting room, Bella plunged a hand into her

dance bag to get her hairbrush. "Oh—ick!" she squealed. She pulled out her hand, and Ellie saw that it was covered with white goo. All the girls stared at it, wide-eyed.

"Oh, no, did something leak in there? That smells like hand lotion," Ellie said.

"It *is* hand lotion, but it's not mine. I didn't bring any today," Bella said. "Somebody squirted it all over my stuff, though. On purpose!"

"But—but why?" Ellie asked. All around her, girls were opening their bags to check for damage.

"They didn't get me," Michelle reported, a funny look on her face. "What about you guys?"

"I'm fine," "Me too," "Nothing here," came the assorted answers.

"What about you, Ellie?" Bella asked. "Did they get you?"

"Me?" Suddenly, Ellie remembered her sweater—her brand-new birthday sweater—folded safely away in her dance bag. Or *was* it still safe? Slowly, she unzipped the bag and looked inside. "Oh, no," she gasped.

All around Ellie, girls craned their necks to peer inside her bag. "Gross," one said.

Loops and whorls of the oily white lotion festooned Ellie's sweater, seeping into the fluffy wool. Ellie looked up, angry tears in her eyes. "But—but who could have done this?" she asked.

"It must have been someone who sneaked in while we were taking class," one of the girls said. "The waiting room was empty then."

"Someone said they saw Dawn come in," another girl said, excited. "Maybe she saw who did it!"

"You mean Dawn was here?" Ellie asked, frowning.

"I heard she went into the office, with her mom," the girl said. "Maybe that's why Ms. Hawkins wasn't teaching today," she added.

"You can wear my extra sweatshirt home, Ellie," Bella said. "It wasn't in my dance bag, it's okay. Do you think we should go tell Ms. Hawkins that someone did this?" Ellie nodded, grim.

"But, Ellie," Bella said, suddenly changing her mind, "she might just tell us not to bother her with our personal problems."

"Well, I'm bothering her," Ellie said, getting up. She thought she already knew exactly what had happened, though; Ellie was sure Dawn herself had been the culprit. This was just Dawn's style.

And Ellie didn't feel sorry for her anymore.

"Leticia Elena, I'm really shocked this incident happened," Ms. Hawkins said, "but we can't keep constant watch over the waiting room. You must understand that."

"I know," Ellie said, "but I'm not saying you have to keep watch. I only wanted to know—"

"You asked if Dawn and her mother came in to see me tonight. But don't they deserve some privacy? Does everything around here have to be common knowledge?"

Ellie took a deep breath. It was obvious she wasn't getting anywhere. "Look, Ms. Hawkins," she said finally, "I know Dawn's been—she's been having some problems lately. I just have to know, was she here tonight?"

"But *why* do you have to know that, Leticia?" Ms. Hawkins asked gently. "Surely you can't think that Dawn would vandalize your dance bag."

"And Bella's bag, too," Ellie said.

"Arabella Amory?" Ms. Hawkins asked, her concern obviously growing.

Oh, *now* she was interested, Ellie thought.

"But then why isn't she in here too?" Ms. Hawkins asked.

"Her mother was in a hurry," Ellie said. And Bella was scared to death of Ms. Hawkins, Ellie added to herself. "But I guess the Amorys will be calling you," she added, looking innocent. "They'll probably be pretty upset, once they find out what happened."

Ms. Hawkins clasped her hands together and placed them carefully on one knee. "This is—this is all most unfortunate," she said slowly.

Especially for my sweater, Ellie thought, furious.

"And of course I'll look into it," Ms. Hawkins continued. She sighed, and then looked as though she had reached a decision. "Dawn and her mother did come here for a conference," the teacher said slowly, keeping her voice low. "I don't suppose it would be violating any confidences to tell you that."

"Were they in here together with you the whole time?" Ellie asked.

Ms. Hawkins laughed a little. "Leticia, you sound like Sherlock Holmes. No, as a matter of fact

I spoke to the two of them together first, but then I had a few words alone with Mrs. Upjohn. So Dawn went out to the waiting room," Ms. Hawkins admitted, sounding reluctant. "But just because she had the opportunity doesn't prove that she did anything wrong."

"I know." She did it, though, Ellie thought.

"Leticia," Ms. Hawkins was saying, as if the thought had just struck her, "Dawn's mother was telling me about you two girls being friends, and all. And I was glad to hear that, because Dawn could *use* a friend right now. She seems to be going through an especially rough time lately," the teacher added.

"Mmm," Ellie said. That wasn't any excuse, she thought angrily.

"Now maybe—just maybe, mind you—Dawn got a little upset with you for some reason," Ms. Hawkins continued. "You know, the way friends sometimes do. But wouldn't it be best if you called Dawn on the phone and talked to her about it? Asked her what happened?"

"I guess," Ellie said. "I don't know."

"I'm sure that would be the way to handle it," Ms. Hawkins said. "Maybe it didn't happen exactly as you thought. Perhaps Dawn saw someone else come into the waiting room!"

What a dreamer, Ellie thought.

"Yes," Ms. Hawkins said, sounding more confident now, "I'm certain that's the way to handle it. Direct communication, Leticia. You have her number, of course?"

"My mom has it, anyway," Ellie said.

"Direct communication," Ms. Hawkins repeated. "And I'll look into it from this end, Leticia."

"Okay, good," Ellie said. Then she added, "Um, Ms. Hawkins? Speaking of direct communication . . ." Her voice faded.

"Mmm? What is it, dear?"

Ellie blurted out her question: "Is it true that Anne Marie Leone is getting married?"

Ms. Hawkins stared at Ellie, then burst out laughing. "Getting married? Wherever did you hear that? My goodness, the rumor mill is certainly working overtime around here."

"But—but why is she quitting dance, then?"

"Well, why don't you call her yourself and ask?" Ms. Hawkins said, tilting her head. "Tell you what, I'll give you Anne Marie's phone number, and you can call her after you call Dawn." She flipped through a file and bent to scribble down a number. "Here," she said, handing it to Ellie. "Find out for yourself, Leticia. That's the only way, to hear it with your own ears."

The shape of my mouth is okay, I guess, but my lips look all creasy in my mom's magnifying mirror. I hate the way they look. For advance self-improvement: Rub on lip balm and stop scrunching up my lips.

—To be continued.

8 Ellie's Mouth

Oh, why had she asked that question about Anne Marie? Ellie blushed as she waited for the bus.

The truth was, though, she had been thinking of the older girl all through class, even when Dawn was busy ruining her birthday sweater in the waiting room. Why was Anne Marie quitting dance?

Maybe she was going to be a model, Ellie thought now, resting her dance bag on her feet to protect it from the damp pavement. She could just see Anne Marie in a magazine, or on MTV. Well, maybe not barefoot, with those dancer's feet . . .

The bus squealed to a wheezy halt in front of her, and Ellie got on for the short ride home.

Or Anne Marie could even be on some TV series, Ellie daydreamed as she took a seat. Anne Marie was at least as pretty as the girls who were on TV. Ellie hoped she wasn't really getting married while she was still in high school—that was so boring!

Walking the final blocks to her apartment, Ellie remembered the ruined sweater with reluctance. What was she going to tell her mother? More important, what was she going to say to Dawn? And was she really going to telephone the famous Anne Marie Leone?

"Hello, is Anne Marie there?" Ellie couldn't believe what she was doing.

"She's out," a boy said. "Can I take a message?"

"Oh, sure," Ellie said, trying to think of what to say next. "Um, would you tell her Ellie Lane called? From ballet? I—I need to interview Anne Marie for, um, for my school paper. I go to Ben Franklin." Well, she did have an English assignment due fairly soon.

"You want to interview her?" The boy sounded impressed.

"Yes, would you tell her?" Ellie said, feeling more confident. "Ms. Hawkins gave me your phone number." Ellie hoped that Ms. Hawkins's magic name would convince Anne Marie to cooperate. "I was hoping maybe the interview could be tomorrow? After company class?" Everything she was saying sounded like a question.

"I'll tell her. You want to leave a phone number?"

"No," Ellie said hurriedly. She didn't want to give Anne Marie the chance to tell her to get lost. "No," she continued, slower now, "I'll just stop by the studio tomorrow. She can tell me in person."

"Well, okay," the boy said. "But wait—who did you say you are? I have to write it down."

"Ellie Lane," Ellie said slowly. "Ms. Hawkins calls me Leticia Elena, though. But probably Anne Marie has never heard of me."

"I'll tell her anyway."

"Hello, Mrs. Upjohn? Is Dawn there? It's Ellie." Dinner was over, and the dishes were done. Ellie had calmed down a little, but she knew she had to confront Dawn now, even though she was a little frightened of the anger Dawn had shown. But if she didn't call tonight, maybe she never would, Ellie thought. And her phone call to Anne Marie—well, to Anne Marie's house—had gone pretty well, so . . .

"Oh, hello, Ellie," Mrs. Upjohn said. "She's up in her room—I'll go get her."

Ellie waited for a minute or two; she could hear voices raised in argument at the Upjohns' house, but she couldn't make out what they were saying.

Finally, Mrs. Upjohn picked up the phone again. "Ellie? Dawn says she—she can't come to the phone right now. Can she call you back?"

Oh, sure, like she was really going to return the call, Ellie thought. "No, that's okay," she said. "Would you go tell her I'll wait here on the phone until she can talk? Tell her if she can't come to the phone, I'll just give the complete message to you," she added. That ought to get some action, she thought.

"Well, all right, Ellie, I'll try one more time," Mrs. Upjohn said.

In a couple of minutes, another voice spoke: "Okay, what?" It was Dawn. She sounded ready to fight.

"Oh, *hi*, Dawn," Ellie said, her voice polite in an exaggerated way. Her heart was pounding, though. "Thanks for deciding to talk to me."

"What do you want, anyway?"

"Well, I heard you came by the ballet studio tonight with your mother. I just wanted to say I'm sorry I missed you."

"How did you know I was there?"

"Oh, you know ballet. Nothing stays secret for long. And anyway, you left a trail behind you."

"What do you mean, a trail?"

Ellie ignored Dawn's question. "That was a mean thing to do, Dawn," she said, "no matter what you think your excuse is."

"You don't know anything, and you can't prove it either," Dawn said, defiant.

"I know you were alone in the waiting room while we were all taking class."

"Big deal—that doesn't prove a thing," Dawn repeated. "Anyway, we *all* carry hand lotion with us. There's no way you can trace it to me."

"Dumb one, Dawn. Who said anything about hand lotion?"

There was a pause; then Dawn spoke again. Her voice sounded harsh now, scornful. But there was a question in it, too. "So what are you going to do about it, anyway? Tell?"

"Yes, unless you pay the dry-cleaning bill for my

sweater. My mom says it could be ten bucks, by the time they finish."

"And what if I don't?" Dawn said. Her voice trembled a little.

"I'll tell Ms. Hawkins that I know for sure you did it."

"And then what do you think will happen?" Dawn asked, beginning to sound sarcastic.

"Well," Ellie said, trying to think fast, "for one thing, I don't think she'll want you trying out on Saturday. Company members are supposed to work together, not play dirty tricks on each other."

"Oh, like you're so sure you'd get in," Dawn said. "I thought you weren't even trying out."

"I said *maybe* I wouldn't, but that's not the point," Ellie said.

"The point *is*," Dawn said, "I don't care if you tell Hawkins or not. She already said I can't audition— you'll be glad to know!" And with that, Dawn burst into noisy, gulping sobs.

"Dawn, wait," Ellie said, suddenly confused. "What on earth are you talking about?"

"Oh, don't pretend like you really care," Dawn managed to say. "Anyway, you know you're a better dancer than me."

"I am not," Ellie said.

"You are too," Dawn said angrily. "Everyone's better than me."

"No, no, you're really good," Ellie heard herself say. Hey, she wondered, what had happened? *She* was supposed to be mad at Dawn, not the other way around!

"Well, but Ms. Hawkins says that doesn't—even—matter," Dawn said, gasping for breath.

"*What* doesn't matter?" Ellie asked, still confused. She felt as though her head was spinning, just like in the cartoons.

"How good a dancer I am," Dawn explained. "Ms. Hawkins says my mental health comes first. Oh, this is all my mother's fault," she added. "She's driving me crazy!"

"Your mother? But why—what did she do?" Ellie asked. This phone call wasn't going at all the way she'd planned.

Dawn sniffed. "Oh, my mom kept me home from dance on Monday, just because I was crying in school, and stuff. Then she called Ms. Hawkins that night and told her about—about my counseling appointments."

"But what—"

"My mom's got this theory that if it wasn't for dance, I wouldn't be so depressed. She thinks without it I'd be fine. She says I'm messing myself up because I spend too much time in a leotard, looking in the mirror, and that's what makes me so hard on myself. What a joke—like I need a reason!"

"Well, is that what your—um, counselor thinks too?" Ellie asked.

Dawn blew her nose. "Not necessarily," she finally said, "but she does think I need a break from my extracurricular activities," she said, mimicking the woman. "She thinks I should see *her* more often, instead. Surprise, surprise."

"But you—"

"Look," Dawn interrupted, "I don't know why I'm so goofed up lately, but dance is about the only thing keeping me sane! Why can't anyone see that?"

Ellie could see it. In fact, she felt that way herself, sometimes. "But I don't get it," she said. "What happened with Ms. Hawkins?"

Dawn took a deep, shaky breath, and then—calmer—she said, "Oh, Hawkins believed them, naturally. Who's going to listen to a kid?"

"And she said you couldn't audition?"

"Basically," Dawn said.

"What did she say, *exactly?*"

"That I could audition separately for her at the end of the summer, if I kept on with my stupid counseling and if it was okay with everyone. Not that it's any of your business," Dawn added, a little of her old spirit coming back.

"Well, that's not so bad, is it?" Ellie asked. "That means Ms. Hawkins really does want you to audition, Dawn. I can't see her doing that for anyone else."

"I guess not," Dawn admitted. "But everyone will wonder, when I don't show up on Saturday. God, I hate my mother!"

"But Dawn, even if your mom was wrong about ballet causing the—the problem," Ellie said, fumbling for the right word, "she must have thought she was doing the right thing."

"Don't defend her," Dawn said fiercely. "Anyway, she's just jealous because she was such a lousy dancer.

Why can't she be more like your mom, all supportive and everything? You have all the luck!"

Yeah, right, Ellie thought.

"So now you're going to go tell everyone, aren't you?" Dawn said, sounding hopeless. "I guess I wouldn't blame you," she added reluctantly.

"Well, I'm still kind of mad," Ellie said. "But what I don't get is why you played such a dirty trick in the first place."

"I don't exactly know," Dawn admitted, sounding exhausted. "I was just sitting there in the waiting room, and then all of a sudden I thought of you and Bella. You guys have everything. Well, between you, you do— she's got the money, and you've got the talent and looks. You never have to worry about stuff or ask any questions. Good things just happen to you, don't they?"

"No, they don't, Dawn. They—"

"Admit it, Ellie! You never have to look at your body in the mirror and try to figure out what's wrong, like I do. It just finally got to me, I guess."

"You really think I'm pretty?" Ellie asked. She was amazed.

"Oh, come on," Dawn said, disgusted. "Stop fishing for compliments. Anyway, so I took the lotion from Michelle's bag and—and I just did it, that's all. And now I'm sorry, okay?"

"Okay," Ellie said slowly. "But—but look. I'm not as sure of myself as you think. I don't know where you got that idea."

"Oh, come on," Dawn repeated. "I can tell just by looking at you."

"But I—"

"I can *tell*, Ellie."

"Huh," Ellie said, giving up for now. "But I still think you ought to pay for cleaning my new sweater, Dawn."

"I didn't know it was new," Dawn said, as if that might be an excuse.

"Well, it was."

"So if I give you the ten dollars, you won't tell anyone?"

"Well, I guess—I guess I was going to tell, but now I won't. I promise I'll keep my mouth shut even if you *don't* give me the ten dollars," Ellie said.

"Why? Because you feel all sorry for me?" Dawn asked, fresh anger in her voice.

"Kind of," Ellie admitted, "but also because we— well, we've known each other since we were little kids. Maybe we're not best friends, but we were almost friends, once." And maybe she and Dawn had more in common than she'd wanted to admit, Ellie added to herself. Staring into the mirror at night . . .

"That was a long time ago, *Leticia*," Dawn said.

Dawn was actually teasing her! That was a pretty good sign. "But okay," Dawn was saying, "I'll give you the money."

"I also think you should stop being so mean to Bella," Ellie said. "She never did anything bad to you. And she has her own problems."

"Oh, sure she does," Dawn said, obviously skeptical. "But what makes you think I'll even be coming back to dance at all, assuming my mother ever lets me?" she asked. "Maybe I don't want to face everyone. All that stupid gossip!"

Yeah, and Dawn was usually the one spreading it around, Ellie thought. It kind of served her right. "Look," she said aloud, "of course you should come back to class. The gossip won't be so bad, not for long, anyway."

"That's what *you* think," Dawn said, but at least she was listening.

"Regular classes will be over pretty soon, when school ends," Ellie continued, "and then a whole new summer program will start. You'll have to keep taking class if you want to audition later." It was true; if a dancer at that level stopped dancing for even a week, it could take up to three weeks to get back in shape.

"And you really think I should audition later?" Dawn asked.

"Yeah, if you decide you still want to," Ellie said. "You're really good, Dawn. You must know that."

"Thanks," Dawn said. "I know you don't mean it, but it's nice to hear anyway."

To her surprise, though, Ellie realized she *did* mean it. And it wouldn't be too terrible if she and Dawn both got into the company. After all, what fun would it be without Dawn to compete against—and to complain about?

"Did she admit she did it?" Ellie's mom asked, standing in the living room doorway.

Ellie nodded. "And she said she'd pay the cleaning bill, too."

Her mother came into the room cradling a pair of soft leather dance shoes. "I sewed the elastic on," she said, holding them out like a peace offering.

Ellie knew her mother was trying to make up for not believing her at first about Dawn's dirty trick. "Dawnie would never," Mrs. Lane had said at dinner. "It must have been another girl, someone who's jealous of you."

"It was Dawn," Ellie had stated flatly.

Now Ellie's mother didn't know what to say. "But—but why?" she finally asked.

"She says all of a sudden she just got jealous of Bella and me," Ellie said.

"Oh, you mean because Bella is your friend now? Ellie, I *told* you we should have invited Dawnie to your party. Poor little thing, she—"

"No, Mom!" Ellie said. "She's not jealous that Bella and I are friends, and she probably never even heard about the party. She was . . . just plain jealous, okay? And like you said, she's depressed. Maybe she was acting weird because of that."

"But did she say anything about the company audition, sweetie?"

"Well," Ellie said reluctantly, "she said Ms. Hawkins told her she had to put off trying out until late in the summer. I guess they're all pretty worried about her."

"It's probably for the best," her mother said, nodding her head. "Her emotional state is more important, after all. And Ellie . . ."

"What, Mom?"

"I hate to say it, I really do, but this will probably work out to your advantage at the audition on Saturday."

"Mom!"

"Well, let's be realistic, darling. Dawn was your competition, basically. So everything has really worked out for the best, for all concerned."

"I can't believe you'd actually say that. It's so—so *cold*." Ellie's mouth felt stiff; she could barely form the words.

"Sweetie, you know I love Dawnie," Mrs. Lane said, trying to soothe her daughter. "I didn't mean anything bad."

"Well, I don't want any part of it, if dance is so competitive," Ellie said, her voice quavering. "How are you supposed to learn how to be an artist, anyway, if you're always thinking ugly thoughts about everyone else?"

Mrs. Lane looked distressed. "Ellie, you don't—"

"No, Mom, *you* don't," Ellie said, trying to control her voice. "You don't get to tell me everything has worked out for the best. You don't even tell me I have to audition. I don't *have* to be a dancer just because you want me to be one!"

Ellie's mother gripped the back of a chair until her hands looked white. "Young lady, you are auditioning on Saturday, and that's final," she said.

"What are you going to do, march me down there with a police escort? *Make* me dance?" Ellie backed slowly across the room as she spoke.

"You're getting hysterical, Ellie," her mother said, reaching out a shaking hand. "Pull yourself together. If you could see your face!"

"What's the matter, is it ugly? *Ugly?*" Ellie shouted. "Just like you?"

"Young lady, that's enough. You—"

"Yes, that *is* enough! I'm going to my room! And just leave—me—alone!"

I don't even want to think about my mom anymore. I'll look at my back, instead. It's kind of hard to see, even looking over my shoulder into the full-length mirror. Hey, maybe Dawn is doing the same thing right now! Weird thought. Not that I'm as messed up as she is about the way I look. Well, here's what I see when I look at my back in the mirror: pale skin with some freckles (oh, great) and a few ribs when I bend over. Hey, I almost look skinny when I do that. Too bad I can't walk around backwards for the rest of my life. Advance self-improvement for my future back: Keep scrubbing with that long-handled brush, and stay thin. Maybe stop eating french fries, except on weekends? Give it serious consideration, anyway.

—To be continued.

9
Ellie's Back

"Hey," Case whispered in English class, "I have to talk to you at lunch. It's about Lily."

"Lily, your sister?" Ellie asked, startled. She and Case had been avoiding each other ever since her birthday party. Maybe Case was sorry he'd held her hand in the first place, Ellie had started to think—or maybe it had meant nothing to him! She had begun to dread English, their one class together.

But at least Ned was at lunch. Things seemed almost normal when he was around. Lunch made Ellie a little homesick for the good old days when she was just twelve. Before she and Case had held hands . . .

But now here was Case, whispering about Lily. Ellie had met Lily a couple of times and had really liked her. "Why?" she asked. "Lily's okay, isn't she?"

"Oh, she's fine. It's just—"

"Casey? Ellie?" Ms. Yardley said. "Do you mind, please? I need to finish up these conferences." A few kids laughed, and Ellie ducked her head, blushed, and stared hard at her notebook. Ms. Yardley—bouncy, energetic, and kind—was one of her favorite teachers, and Ellie didn't want to make her angry.

Today, Thursday, Ms. Yardley was finishing up talking to her students individually about their final work for the class newspaper. Typically, she had started on Wednesday with the N–Z kids. "They always have to wait," she'd pointed out.

So today was A–M, which included "Hill" and "Lane." "Ellie Lane?" Ms. Yardley called out as Tracy Kaplan took her seat. "Bring your notes, please."

Ellie snapped open her notebook, took out a piece of paper, and hurried to the front of the class. Silently, she handed the paper over to Ms. Yardley. The teacher bent her dark curls over the paper and quickly read it. "An interview. Interesting idea, Ellie," she said.

"Thanks."

"And how old is this girl?"

"I think she's seventeen. Maybe I could even get a photo of her. She's really pretty."

"That would be great—we need more photographs in the paper. But what do you think about doing more than just the one interview?"

"What do you mean?" Ellie asked.

"Well, we have four more class newspapers to get out, and I think this is such a good idea that you could easily expand upon it, maybe add to your article with entries from that diary you told me you were keeping."

"Well, maybe," Ellie said, looking doubtful. She thought about parts of her diary and had to swallow a giggle. *My rear end*, she thought. That would make interesting reading.

"For instance," Ms. Yardley continued, "how about interviewing someone who's just starting out in dance? Do you know any little kids?"

"I—I kind of know one," Ellie said slowly, thinking of Lily Hill. "Case's sister just started pre-ballet after Christmas."

"Is she a good talker?" Ms. Yardley asked.

"Yes," Ellie said. Boy, that was the understatement of the year.

"Good. And then what about somebody older, someone who used to take ballet? It would be interesting to hear what they had to say."

"I guess maybe my ballet teacher would . . ."

"Excellent," Ms. Yardley said. "That just leaves one more, then."

"One more? But who—"

"You, Ellie. You! I want you to interview yourself.

Tell us all how *you* feel about dancing. It'll be fascinating."

Yeah, Ellie thought, making her way back to her seat. Fascinating.

But first she had to figure out how she *did* feel about dance.

"So did you get in trouble for talking in class?" Case asked at lunch. Things seemed almost magically back to normal between them—maybe she had Lily to thank for that. And Ned hadn't even shown up yet.

"No, she didn't mention it again," Ellie said. "She was too busy throwing assignments at me."

"For the paper? Why, what are you going to do?"

"Interviews," Ellie said. "As a matter of fact, she wants me to interview Lily."

"You're kidding. Why?"

"Because she's just starting out in ballet. Do you think Lily would mind?"

"Are you kidding?" he repeated. "Lily mind talking about herself? Her only problem is, she thought she was going to be able to dance as soon as she put on the right clothes, so she's about ready to quit. But she'll talk to you. She thinks you're like this goddess," Case said, laughing. "In fact, I was going to ask if you could babysit for her tomorrow night. My mom wants to know."

"Tomorrow night?" Ellie said slowly. "Let me think . . ." That was the night before the audition, she thought. But was she even going to the audition?

"Mom wants to go out to dinner with some friend," Case was saying, "and I'm supposed to help set up for this fund-raiser at the antique store. So *I* can't sit."

"Well, maybe I could," Ellie said, not wanting to disappoint him, "but I know my parents would say it has to be at my place. That's one of their many rules— even though I'm thirteen," she added, disgusted.

"That's okay," Case said. "I could bring her over on the bus, and then my mom will pick her up. What time do you get home from dance?"

"I can make it there by seven, if I hurry," Ellie said.

"And my mom will come get her by nine-thirty, at the latest. Hey—maybe you can interview Lily tomorrow. Kill two birds with one stone."

If my mom doesn't kill me first, Ellie thought. She was supposed to ask permission in advance. Well, she was already in so much trouble . . .

"So are you coming to chess club after school today?" Case was asking.

"Uh, only for a little while," Ellie said. "Just to watch. Then I have to go over to the ballet studio for something."

"You sure spend a lot of time there," Case said.

"I know. It's like this whole way of life," Ellie said, bitterly echoing what her mother sometimes said— only when her mom said it, she meant ballet was like heaven.

"You don't sound too happy about it."

"Well, I love it and I hate it. It's—it's hard to explain."

"Oh," Case said.

He sounded confused, Ellie thought. But he wasn't as confused about it as she was, she added to herself. On bad days, Ellie felt that she was dancing only because her mother wanted her to. It was as though she was a ballerina puppet, almost. Sometimes Ellie even felt she *was* her mother, her young, dancing mother. That was on bad days.

On good days, though, Ellie wasn't at all confused about ballet. It was the thing she most loved doing in the whole wide world. She liked the sound of the piano, the quiet of the studio, the feeling that her body would do exactly what she expected of it—and the awareness that it might do what she hadn't known it could. She even liked feeling tired after class; it was a *good* tired.

On good days, Ellie felt more like herself in ballet class than she did anywhere else in the world.

"Leticia Elena," Ms. Hawkins said, "Anne Marie told me you'd be stopping by to talk to her today, but she's in class for another forty-five minutes, dear."

"I decided to come in early to—to get my questions ready," Ellie said.

In fact, she had most of them written down already, but she'd left chess club even earlier than she planned. When she walked into the room, Mr. Branowski—the club's coach—had looked up from his game, frowned, and said, "Oh, look, Ellie's back!" in a sarcastic voice. And she'd always *liked* him.

"It's just because you've missed so many meetings,"

Ned whispered, taking her aside. "It goofs up his plans."

"I don't *want* to miss chess club, but sometimes I have to," Ellie said, thinking of all the extra ballet classes Ms. Hawkins had called over the last two months.

"Yeah, but that still means he has to change things around so everyone has someone to play," Ned pointed out.

"I guess I should apologize," Ellie said.

"Maybe, but not today. He's kind of in a bad mood."

"Yeah, I noticed," Ellie had said, and she'd slipped out the door.

Now Ellie had an idea. "Um, Ms. Hawkins?"

The teacher looked up from her desk. Ellie thought again how expressive her teacher's eyes were, how straight her back was. She looked like a dancer even when she was sitting still. "Yes, Leticia?"

"I'm sorry to bother you, but you know my English teacher? She asked if I could interview you, too. For our class paper, I mean."

"She wants you to interview me? But why?"

"Well, she thought it would be interesting to have different points of view about dance. Like, I'm going to talk with a little kid who's just starting, and then Anne Marie Leone, who's stopping, and maybe you. I hope."

"Who has already stopped," Ms. Hawkins said.

"Well, stopped performing, anyway," Ellie said,

looking up at the dance posters that showed Ms. Hawkins in some of her earlier roles. "And then I guess I'm supposed to interview myself, too." But she was going to have to save that story for last, she thought. She didn't know how that story was going to end up, yet.

Ms. Hawkins stood up. "I'd be happy to talk with you, Leticia. Why don't we do it now?"

"Now?"

"Come on back to the conference room."

The so-called conference room was a small, crowded space behind the waiting room. Ellie fumbled with her notebook and pen as she sat down on the room's one small sofa. What was she going to ask her teacher?

But Ms. Hawkins made it easy. "I grew up in Louisville, Kentucky, and I started dancing when I was seven," she began. "I studied at the academy there. Then I was offered a contract as an apprentice with the Louisville Ballet when I was seventeen. I danced small parts at first—I was basically decorating the wall for a while," she said, laughing. "I was short for a dancer, even on pointe," she added.

"Were you still living with your family then?" Ellie asked.

"Yes, at first, but then I rented an apartment with another girl."

"So how long did it take to start getting better roles?"

"Well, after my apprenticeship, I was in the corps for a couple of years. That's spelled *c-o-r-p-s*, Leticia, but it's pronounced *core*. That's French for 'body.'"

"And then what happened?"

"Then I started to get some attention. A boy joined the company who was a good partner for me, thank heavens. I was eventually promoted to soloist, then to principal dancer. Some of the posters in the waiting room are from that period."

"How old were you then?"

"Twenty-four, twenty-five. It was a wonderful time."

"And then what happened?" Ellie asked.

"Two things, really. First, I started having some trouble with my hip. I'd injured it twice by then. I worked with the physical therapist and so on, but pretty soon it became obvious I was going to have to have surgery. So I took a leave of absence."

"But you dance now, every day in class," Ellie said. "So the operation must have worked. Didn't you go back to the company?"

Ms. Hawkins slowly shook her head. "No," she said. "They offered me another contract, but I decided not to accept it."

Ellie paused in her note taking and looked up. "But—but why?"

"Because I decided I wanted a different kind of life—a bigger life, in a way. My boyfriend and I had just broken up, and I knew I had to make time for other interests, after I found out what those were. But I knew that I wanted to meet people who weren't necessarily dancers, and that can be hard when you're in the studio all the time."

"But you're still teaching dance," Ellie said, confused.

110

"Leticia, I love ballet," Ms. Hawkins said. "I never wanted to turn my back on it completely."

"But wasn't it hard to stop performing? To give it all up?"

"Well, certainly I miss being able to dance the way I once did, but that happens to every dancer. And I never thought that I was giving anything up, not really."

Ellie's words tumbled out: "But all that work, for nothing!"

"It wasn't for nothing, Leticia. I'd had all those wonderful years of training," her teacher said, "and then another ten years' performing. Do you really call that nothing?"

"I guess not," Ellie said slowly. "But I still think you're good enough to be performing now. Everyone does."

Ms. Hawkins laughed. "Thank you, dear, but I'm very happy right here. I have a wonderful personal life, and I have this school to run. You know I've always told you girls that even if you have a career in dance, you need to prepare for another career as well. No one can dance forever."

"I know," Ellie said. "I just thought—"

"That stopping was the end of the world?"

"For someone like you," Ellie said. "A professional, I mean."

"Well," Ms. Hawkins said, "I won't say it was easy, because it wasn't. I still miss it sometimes, to tell you the truth. But I never lost dance, Leticia. I still have it— all the experiences, the memories, the beauty, not to mention all the things dance gives me now. My entire life has been in dance, and it's been a wonderful life. So don't you dare feel sorry for me."

"Okay, I won't," Ellie said, closing her notebook.

Ms. Hawkins stood up—arose, really, as though she'd been lifted by an invisible string—and said, "Company class is almost out. I'll tell Anne Marie to come in here for her interview, Leticia. You can stay put."

"Okay," Ellie said, nervous once again.

"Oh, and Leticia?" Ms. Hawkins paused at the door. "I really enjoyed this. You're a good reporter!"

"Thanks. And thank you for talking to me," Ellie said.

"Well, dear, see you in class tomorrow. And Saturday, I hope?" But Ellie didn't have a chance to respond; the conference room door had already swung shut.

Anne Marie Leone flopped her legs over the side of the sofa and took a drink from her can of diet cola. Then she looked at Ellie and said, "Go on, ask me anything."

"Why are you quitting?" Ellie blurted out.

Anne Marie threw her head back and laughed. Her long hair—wavy from having been in a bun—almost reached the cushions, Ellie noticed. "Because I want a life!" Anne Marie said.

"A life?" Ellie asked.

"You know, like in senior year? Look. I'm not going to be a professional dancer, right? But I *am* going to be a senior in high school next year, right? So why waste a whole other year being in dance when I could be out there enjoying myself! Not to mention spending more time on my studies."

"But—but can't you do both? All three things, I mean."

"Sure you can, just not very well. And that's what I've been doing. It's time for a change, that's all. I want to be able to go to a friend's house after school—instead of taking class. Paint my fingernails red for once—instead of always keeping them bare. Join school clubs if I want to. Eat an ice cream cone without feeling guilty. Date! I'm tired of saying, 'I can't, I have ballet class,' 'I can't, I have a rehearsal.' That's been my motto, practically. Hey, I'm just plain tired!"

"Uh, when did you decide you wanted to quit?" Ellie asked, scribbling fast.

"Last Christmas," Anne Marie said promptly. "We had all those extra rehearsals, and I had to miss this school dance I really wanted to go to. Not to mention a couple of parties. My boyfriend was *mad*. And I thought, do I really want to go through another whole year like this one?"

"But how come you stayed in dance for so long, if you hated it so much?"

"Oh, I didn't hate it. But I don't know why I stayed. It wasn't my mom or dad—it was always me who had pushed for it, right from the start. They didn't mind, though. Maybe they thought it would keep me out of trouble! Anyway, I was good at dance, and I liked the attention. It was good for my insecurity, I guess."

Insecurity, Ellie thought, stunned. That should be her headline: EXTRA! EXTRA! *Anne Marie Leone Actually Feels Insecure About Something!*

"Um, insecurity?" Ellie asked aloud, trying not to sound too curious.

"Sure," Anne Marie said, and she laughed. "You know, about my body, my hair. The usual, only with dance thrown on top of everything—kind of like a magnifying glass. But maybe you don't worry about stuff like that," she said, pausing to look quizzically at Ellie.

"Oh, I worry," Ellie said. And that could be the understatement of the *century*, she thought.

"But I'm not saying I'm not going to miss dance," Anne Marie continued. "I will. Hey, it's a habit. It'll probably be a tough one to break, too—not that I'm going to stop completely."

"What do you mean?" Ellie asked.

"Oh, I'll probably always take some kind of dance," Anne Marie said, "once I get rested up. A couple of times a week, anyway. For *fun*," she stressed, as if trying out a new idea. "What about you?" she added suddenly.

"Me?"

"I heard you're pretty good. Are you trying out for the company?"

"I—I don't know yet. My mother really wants me to," Ellie said.

"Well, don't do it for *her*," Anne Marie advised. "Tell her to get a life of her own."

Sure, Ellie thought.

Anne Marie looked at her watch and jumped up.

"Jason is probably waiting," she said, her smile suddenly shy. "My boyfriend. We're going out tonight—to celebrate."

"Is it your birthday?" Ellie asked.

Anne Marie laughed again as she straightened her sweater. "Nope. It was my last ballet class!"

"Oh, by the way," Ellie said, "do you have a picture I can use with the article? A snapshot maybe?"

"Sure. I'll mail it in here to the office—I don't want to come back here until I'm good and ready. Bye, Ellie. And good luck—with everything."

"Thanks." She was going to need it.

Green eyes, dark lashes. Thank goodness,
because I know my mom wouldn't let me wear
makeup in public yet: oh, no, ballerinas have to
be different. But are my lashes thick enough?
Models always talk about thick eyelashes, like
your body is supposed to figure out, "Everywhere
else thin, but not here." Right. My eyebrows
look a little hairy to me, but I don't want to end
up with those creepy wiggly brows you get
when you thin them too much. Which I probably
would, knowing me. No, my eyes are okay,
really. They're maybe even my best feature, if
that's not bragging. Not that anyone else will
ever read this. Sorry, Ms. Yardley!
　　—To be continued.

10
Ellie's Eyes

Bella didn't show up for Level Six that Friday, and neither did Dawn. Ellie searched the bare, mirrored room as she gripped the barre. Mrs. Fiori looked up from the piano and gave her a smile.

"And—finish," Ms. Hawkins said. The girls resumed their original positions. "And the other side," the ballet teacher continued.

Ellie lost herself in concentration as she carried out the exercise. The familiar movements, the piano, Ms. Hawkins's voice, the thumping of her silver-topped cane, even the time of day—all these things blended together to create a feeling Ellie loved. This place really *was* home.

"Left hand, Leticia Elena," Ms. Hawkins said, right behind her. "You're not on a roller coaster, you don't need to hold on to the barre for dear life."

That showed how much *she* knew, Ellie thought.

Lily Hill sat cross-legged on Ellie's bed. Ellie's mom and dad had hurried home from an early dinner together—which shocked Ellie when she heard about it—so that they would be at the apartment when the little girl arrived. "If you had a little sister, would you want her to be me?" she asked, watching Ellie brush her hair. In spite of rushing home from dance with her hair still up in a bun, Ellie had missed being there when Case dropped Lily off.

She'd missed him! And seeing him again was what she'd been looking forward to. Now she'd have to wait until Monday.

Ellie yanked at the hairbrush grouchily. "Sure, I guess so," she said to Lily.

"Doesn't it hurt when you do that?" Lily asked, wide-eyed.

"You have to suffer to be beautiful," Ellie answered, joking. But when she saw that Lily believed her, she said, "I was only kidding about that. Hey, did you eat yet?"

"My mom gave me dinner. Macaroni and cheese," Lily reported. "We almost have the same name, don't we? Lily and Ellie, Lily-and-Ellie."

"They are kind of the same," Ellie said.

"Like sisters!"

Ellie laughed. "Come on into the kitchen, and I'll grab a bite. I'm starving. Hey, it sounds like you're feeling kind of cheated that you have a brother and not a sister," she teased, opening the refrigerator. Maybe she could get Lily to talk about Case, at least.

"Oh, Case is okay," Lily said, "except he's bossy sometimes. And he doesn't like to do any fun stuff," she continued, watching Ellie make a sandwich.

"Like what?"

"Oh, like play with my dolls," Lily said. "I brought a couple over," she added, sounding a little uncertain. "You want to play later?"

Ellie had seen the little suitcase Lily had brought with her. "Sure," she said. Relieved, Lily watched her chew for a moment. "Can we make popcorn, too?"

"Okay," Ellie said. "After the dolls."

"And then can we try on makeup? Let's pretend we're really sisters, okay?"

"Well, I'm not so sure about the makeup, Lily. What would your mom say?" Lily was only what, seven?

"She wants me to have fun," Lily said promptly. "And Case doesn't have any makeup. This might be my only chance."

"Well, maybe," Ellie said. "Anyway, it all washes off. So we'll do dolls, popcorn, and makeup?"

"Yeah," Lily said. "Are you almost done with that sandwich?"

Ellie carefully applied blusher on the little girl's round cheeks. "More!" Lily said, looking in the mirror.

"You don't want *too* much, or you'll look like a— You'll look funny," Ellie said.

"Okay, but can't you at least cover up my freckles?" Lily asked.

"I'll use some liquid makeup for that." Ellie selected a bottle from the small collection of cosmetics her mother had given her to experiment with. "You don't need much," she repeated.

"But I want lots!"

"Okay, okay," Ellie said, and she dabbed on a little more, smoothing it out with her finger.

"Now you," Lily commanded.

Ellie rubbed a little of the makeup on her nose; then she applied the blusher. "How's that?"

"Good. Now for our eyes. I want to look like *that*." Lily pointed to a nearby magazine picture.

"Okay, I'll try," Ellie said. "Let's see, I guess I'll start with the eye shadow." Lily raised her head and squinched her eyes shut. "Just relax your eyes, Lily, or I won't be able to do it." Lily's little jaw sagged open as she tried to cooperate. "That's better," Ellie said, trying not to laugh.

She brushed and blended three colors of shadow onto Lily's eyelids. "Let me see. Let me see!" Lily demanded.

"Okay, but I'm not done yet." Ellie held up the mirror. "What about my eyelashes? Can't you make them bigger?"

"Well, I can make them darker, but I don't have any false lashes."

"How come?" Lily wanted to know.

"Where would I wear them? To school?"

"I'm going to, when I'm a teenager," Lily said, looking a little disappointed. "That's what I want to be when I grow up—a teenager. And I'm going to wear lots of makeup, all the time. And I'm going to have big eyelashes, too."

Ellie bit her lower lip, thinking. Was this such a great thing she was doing? "Close your eyes again—I'm going to use an eyeliner pencil now," she said, giving in with a sigh. "It'll feel weird, I'm warning you. So what else are you going to do when you're a teenager?" Ellie asked. She almost didn't want to know.

"That does feel weird," Lily said. "I'm going to be a ballerina, just like you, and a cheerleader. And I'm going to have lots of different outfits."

"Like your dolls?" Ellie asked, smiling. Lily nodded violently. "Hey, watch it. Hold still," Ellie said.

"Just like my dolls. Only my stuff will be bigger."

"Good idea," Ellie said. "Almost finished. Do you want mascara?"

"Of course."

Of course! "Okay, but you'll have to hold very still for that. I don't want to jab you in the eye," Ellie said. "I hope your mom doesn't freak," she added, almost to herself.

"Oh, she never freaks," Lily said. "That tickles!"

"Hold still," Ellie repeated.

"I wish my daddy could see me, though," Lily said.

Her daddy, Ellie thought, holding her breath for a moment—her daddy in prison. Was Lily going to talk about it? "Well, maybe we can take a picture of you," Ellie suggested, "and you can send it to him." If there was any film in the camera, she thought.

"Really?" Lily squealed.

"Hold *still*," Ellie said again. "I don't want to poke your eye out."

"That's okay," Lily joked. "I guess I have to suffer if I want to be beautiful!"

"I said I was kidding about that," Ellie said, much alarmed. "But that reminds me—can I ask you some questions about dance? It's for this assignment in English. Case told me you started pre-ballet after Christmas." She started applying the makeup to her own face.

Lily nodded. "But I don't get to wear a tutu yet. I thought I would."

"What do you wear?"

"Black leotard, pink tights, pink shoes," Lily reported. "Same as the big girls," she added, her voice brightening.

"And how do you like it so far?"

"It's boring—I wanted to wear something else."

"No, I mean dance. How do you like ballet?"

Lily shrugged. "It's okay, I guess. But Ms. Hawkins is really strict. We have to stand perfectly still, and listen." Lily made it sound as though they'd been asked to eat snails—raw. "And some of it is in French," she said, outraged.

"Well, do the other kids like it?"

"Yeah, but a couple of them look kind of dumb. Like this one girl? Her tummy sticks way out. Ms. Hawkins told her to hold in some of that hamburger."

Ellie winced, recognizing the phrase. And the poor kid was so young!

"And right before Easter?" Lily continued. "Right when we were leaving, Ms. Hawkins told us not to eat too many chocolate bunnies. And that's the whole point about Easter. Duh!"

"So did you eat any chocolate bunnies?"

"No," Lily said, looking crafty, "but I ate a ton of jellybeans."

"What about your mom?" Ellie asked. "Was it her idea for you to take dance?"

"No, it was mine. My best friend started taking it first. But then she stopped."

"How come?"

"Oh, she wanted to try karate instead."

"So are you going to take karate too?"

"I might," Lily said. "You get to make some noise, anyway. Eee-*YAH!*"

Ellie jumped, and they both laughed.

"But I guess I'll keep on dancing," Lily continued. "I want to be just like you," she added shyly.

"So who are these beautiful ladies?" Ellie's father said, pushing the TV remote's mute button.

"I'm a model, and Ellie is a cheerleader," Lily said. "We're sisters!"

"You look wonderful," Ellie's mom said. "So elegant. And look at Ellie's eyes."

"It's no big deal, Mom," Ellie said. "But where's the camera? Lily wanted me to take a picture."

"For my daddy," the little girl added.

"It's over there, on top of my desk," Mrs. Lane said. "See it?"

"Let me take a picture of the two of you together," Ellie's father said.

"Can I keep that one, too?" Lily asked.

"Sure, if it comes out," Ellie said. Maybe Case would see it, she thought. She wouldn't mind that at all. She did look pretty good . . .

"Okay, girls, stand over there, next to the curtains. Now, smile!"

Mrs. Hill was right on time, much to Lily's disappointment. "Well, don't you look nice," Lily's mother said, raising her eyebrows in surprise.

"I hope it's all right," Ellie said, nervous.

"Me and Ellie played sisters," Lily said. "She's going to send me pictures, for Daddy. And we made popcorn."

"You ladies certainly have been busy. Thanks again, Ellie," Mrs. Hill said, handing her some money.

"Are you going home on the bus?" Ellie asked. "Do you want me to wash Lily's face first?"

"No!" Lily said. "I want to keep it just like this."

"That's okay," Mrs. Hill said. "My friend has a car. He's waiting downstairs."

"Who is it?" Lily asked.

"You'll see," Mrs. Hill said. "We're supposed to swing by and pick up Case, too, so get your things, Lily."

"Case gets to see my new face," Lily said, smiling. "I wonder if he'll recognize me."

"Oh, he's pretty sharp," Mrs. Hill said.

"Now, be sure and scrub your face before you go to bed," Ellie said.

"You mean take the makeup off?" Lily was astounded.

"Sure. That's one of the rules about being beautiful—you always go to sleep with a nice clean face."

"But first you put on moisturizer," Lily added, surprising them all. "It says so on TV."

"What a darling little girl," Ellie's mom said in the kitchen, as Ellie poured herself a glass of orange juice. "It's too bad about her father, though."

"Mmm," Ellie said. She didn't want to talk about Case's father.

"Her mother seems like a lovely woman, doesn't she?"

"I guess," Ellie said. She headed toward the door.

"Is everything all set for the audition tomorrow?" her mother asked brightly. "Did you see the new tights? I put them on your bed."

"I saw them," Ellie said, her voice stony. Her mom

wasn't even asking her if she wanted to audition—she was telling her she had to do it.

Mrs. Lane set down her water glass with a clunk. "Ellie, sweetie, for heaven's sake—talk to me!"

"What do you want me to say, Mother?"

"Tomorrow is a big day for you. You don't want to go into the audition with a frown on your pretty face."

"My pretty face!" Suddenly, Ellie hated the make-up she still wore. She hated the makeup Lily wore! It stood for the worst of what her mother seemed to think was important: so-called beauty. Ellie could almost hear the whine of her mom's salon hair dryers and smell the nail polish remover as she spoke. "You—you *like* me like this, don't you?" Ellie said, her words pouring out. "Like this, but with a smile pasted on? And you're just the same with Daddy. You don't even care what's going on *inside* anyone's head, as long as the outside looks okay."

"Ellie, that's not true. And your father and I—"

"It is *too* true," Ellie interrupted.

"Do you really think I don't care what you're feeling inside?" Mrs. Lane asked. "That's practically *all* I've been thinking about, heaven help me!"

"Well, just don't, Mom," Ellie said. "Just don't."

"Look, Ellie," her mother said, shrugging helplessly, "I know I've made mistakes. But I only wanted you to be able to keep this one beautiful thing in your life, sweetie. You have a chance to be a real dancer."

"I can't help it if *you* didn't have a chance," Ellie said. "I can't change that!"

"But I don't expect you to."

"Oh, yes you do," Ellie said, "and it just—it just makes me tired, that's all. So I'm going to bed early, you'll be glad to hear. To get my beauty sleep!" Ellie cringed when she saw the look on her mother's face. But it served her mom right, she thought. Didn't it?

Ellie's dad poked his head into the kitchen. "What?" Ellie and her mom said, both at the same time.

"Sorry to interrupt," he said mildly, "but there's a phone call for Ellie."

"Who is it?" Ellie's mother asked.

"Mother, that's my business," Ellie said, furious once more.

"Well, don't talk too long," her mother called after her.

I'll talk as long as I want, Ellie thought rebelliously. She didn't say anything, though; she'd already said too much.

"Ellie, it's me. Bella." Her friend's voice sounded far away, and Ellie could hear a car horn honking in the background.

"Where are you? You sound all—funny," Ellie said.

"I'm at the pay phone in front of the video store. You know, where we went on your birthday."

"You are? But it's—it's almost ten," Ellie said, looking at her watch. "Are you with your parents or something?"

"No, they're home. They think I'm with you, as a matter of fact. That's one of the reasons I'm calling."

"But I don't get it. What's going on?"

"I can't go home, Ellie, I'm scared. Can I come over?"

"Well sure, but—" Ellie hesitated, thinking of her angry mother, her bewildered father. "Wait a minute," she said, trying to think. "Want me to come and get you?"

"Could you?"

"Well, wait in the store. I'll—I'll sneak you into the apartment."

"Sneak me in? But why?" Bella asked, confused. "Can't you just ask your mom and dad?"

"It's too complicated to explain," Ellie said. She didn't want to ask them anything, not tonight. "Wait for me," she repeated. "I'll be down as fast as I can."

In another ten minutes, Ellie's parents had gone into their bedroom, shutting the door behind them. Ellie knew they were in there for the night. Waiting a bit longer, she scrubbed her face clean, then she crept out of her room. She walked silently through the darkened apartment; the only lights shone in from outside, making familiar rooms eerie.

Ellie opened the front door as quietly as she could, then snicked it shut softly behind her. She raced down the steps to the front hall, let herself out into the night, and ran to the video store.

Sure enough, there was Bella, pretending to search for a video. She shoved an empty box back onto its shelf when Ellie came through the door.

Bella looked tired and hungry. She was all bundled up in a jacket, and she wore a big, floppy beret.

"What are you doing here, anyway?" Ellie asked, looking around nervously. "No, wait, let's go back to the apartment. You can tell me then."

The two girls let themselves back into the Lanes' building and walked quietly up the stairs. "Shhh," Ellie warned, turning the doorknob as noiselessly as she could. *This way,* she mimed, and the girls tiptoed to Ellie's room. "Phew!" she sighed, once she had shut the door behind them.

"You can say that again," Bella whispered, dropping into a chair. "Can your parents hear us?" she asked.

"No, they're way on the other side," Ellie said. "What about your mother and father, though? They really think you've been here tonight?"

Bella nodded, looking solemn. "I left a note and told them we wanted to go to the audition together tomorrow. I figured my mother would be so glad I was actually going that she wouldn't squawk. She didn't call, did she?"

"No, thank goodness," Ellie said.

"I didn't think she would," Bella said grimly.

"But what's going on? Are you running away or something?" Ellie asked.

"I may have to, after—this," Bella said, and she whipped off her beret.

Arabella had cut off most of her hair!

What do I really want to do? What's in my heart? If I decide to audition, will it just be for my mom's sake—will it be because I'm scared of her? On the other hand, if I <u>don't</u> audition just to teach her a lesson, but I really want to audition, that would be kind of dumb. On the other hand, how do I figure out where what-she-wants stops and where what-I-want starts? Wait—that's three hands, which is one too many.
—To be continued.

11
Ellie's Heart

The hair that was left stood up in little blond tufts on the top of Bella's head. It was longer around her ears and neck, but not by much. "What—what did you do it with?" Ellie asked. She could barely get the words out.

"Nail scissors," Bella said, her voice wobbly. "You know, from my dance bag. It doesn't look *too* bad, does it?"

"When did you do it?" Ellie asked, not answering the question.

"After school, in the girls' bathroom. I stuffed the hair into the trash," she added, "and covered it with paper towels."

"The custodian is probably going to faint when he sees it," Ellie said, and she giggled in spite of everything.

Bella started to laugh too. "Probably," she agreed. "Poor guy."

"But why did you actually *do* it?" Ellie asked. "Was it really just to get out of the audition?"

"Sure," Bella said, running her hands through what was left of her hair, making it stick up even more. Ellie stared, fascinated. "Why else would I do it?" Bella asked.

"I don't know," Ellie said helplessly. "To get back at your mom, maybe. I guess I didn't realize you really hated dance all that much. I mean, you said you didn't want to audition, but . . ." Her voice faded.

"Well, I do hate dance," Bella said, not very convincingly. "I don't want to be in the company. Taking dance was all my mother's idea, right from the start. I heard her tell my dad once that maybe it would teach me to walk across the room without bumping into the furniture." The hurt was still in Bella's voice.

"She actually said that?" Ellie's heart ached for her friend. At least her own parents had never made fun of her!

"Yeah, she did. Daddy was trying to say that maybe I shouldn't take dance if I didn't want to. Anyway, this ought to show her," Bella said with grim satisfaction. Her eyes caught Ellie's, and she looked uncertain again. "I mean, she can't keep on trying to run my life for me, can she?"

"No, I guess not," Ellie said. "But I thought you really *liked* dance, deep down!"

"Well, I like the music," Bella said slowly.

"But not the kids?"

"No, I like the kids okay," Bella admitted. "All except for Dawn, anyway."

"Is it the classes? Ms. Hawkins? What didn't you like?"

"I don't know," Bella wailed, clamping her hands over her ears. "Maybe it was the coach. Stop asking!"

"Okay, I'm sorry," Ellie said, trying to calm her down. "I won't ask. But what are we going to do now?"

"We?" Bella said, lowering her hands. "We?" she repeated.

"I figure I helped get you into this, in a way," Ellie said with a small, tight smile. "I brought up the brilliant bunhead idea in the first place, don't forget."

"But I won't tell," Bella promised. "I'll say I thought the whole thing up. Oh, Ellie," she asked suddenly, "what have I done?"

"It'll grow back," Ellie said, her voice soothing. *Yeah, but when?* she couldn't help asking herself. Right now, Bella looked like a blond hedgehog or something.

"Can I stay here tonight?" Bella begged. "My mother won't go near the dance studio tomorrow—she knows parents aren't allowed at the audition. She won't be expecting me until noon."

"Not that she could do much about it even if she saw you," Ellie said. "You know the bunhead rule."

"Well, I'm not taking any chances. But what about *you*, Ellie? You're not really going to try out, are you?"

"I—I'm still thinking about it," Ellie said slowly. "But one thing's for sure, it's going to be *my* decision. Here's what we'll do first thing tomorrow morning, though. . . ."

The alarm clock went off at five-thirty. Ellie banged it quiet and reached over to turn on the bedside light. She looked over at the still-sleeping Bella; stray blond hairs glinted on her friend's pillow. They must have been stuck to her school sweatshirt, the one she was sleeping in. Bella's chopped-off hair didn't look any better in the morning, although it didn't really seem like morning yet, it was so dark.

"Bella, wake up," Ellie said quietly. "Come on. Get into your clothes."

"Okay, but I have to use the bathroom first," Bella mumbled. The bathroom was down the hall.

"Can't you wait?" Ellie asked. "You might wake up my parents. There's a bathroom where we're going." She climbed out of bed, padded over to her desk, and started rummaging in a drawer for a sheet of notebook paper.

"Oh, I guess I can wait," Bella said, grouchy. She reached up to smooth back her hair and stopped, shocked.

"Your hair is still gone," Ellie said, giving her friend what she hoped was a reassuring grin. She clicked her ballpoint pen a few times, considering.

"It's all coming back to me now," Bella whispered dramatically, as if she were an actress whose character was recovering from amnesia.

"Just let me figure out what to say in this note," Ellie said, "and then we can get dressed and leave. Do you have any money with you?"

"A few dollars," Bella said.

"Good, and I've got my babysitting money. That ought to be enough."

"Enough for what?" Bella asked.

"You'll see," Ellie said. "Now shhh, so I can write."

It was a little after six and still dark when the two girls sneaked out of the Lanes' apartment. Ellie left the note to her mom on the kitchen table:

Dear Mom,

Bella spent the night, in case Mrs. Amory calls. We left early to go out to breakfast.

I'll decide for myself about the audition. I can't do it just for you. But if I decide yes and you come to the ballet studio this morning, I'm leaving. Ms. Hawkins said NO PARENTS.

I will be back this afternoon, one way or the other. I'm sorry if this hurts your feelings, but mine have been hurt too.

Love,
Ellie

Ellie and Bella caught an early bus that headed back across town toward the ballet studio. There was a coffee shop near there that was open twenty-four hours a day.

The bus's softly glowing interior made Ellie feel as if she and Arabella were on an illuminated island that floated through the still-dark city streets. Only a few other passengers rode so early that drizzly Saturday morning; they nodded and dozed, but Ellie and Bella were wide awake. Maybe it was the bright crayon-blue and red seats that did the trick.

"So what's going to happen?" Bella asked, keeping her voice low.

"First we'll use the rest room, then we'll eat. Slowly, to use up time," Ellie said.

"Good plan so far," Bella said, looking hungry.

"The audition goes from nine to about eleven," Ellie continued, "but you're supposed to check in at around eight-fifteen to fill out papers and warm up."

"Ellie, you're actually going to do it?" Bella looked disappointed.

Ellie nodded slowly.

"But why?" Bella wailed. "It would be so great if we both just blew it off! What are you afraid of—your mom?"

"If I was scared of my mother, I wouldn't have left that note," Ellie said. "And I wouldn't have gone sneaking out of the house."

"But you don't want to be in the company, do you?"

"Why not? Hey, I might not even *get* in. But I do know I want to keep on dancing—for now, anyway. It's the best thing in my life."

"But you'll have to take class every single day if you get in," Bella said patiently, still trying to talk her out of it. "And on Saturdays, too! You'll have to quit chess club, you know. You won't get to see Case as often."

"I know," Ellie said. "Don't remind me. Anyway, I can still play chess with Case and Ned on weekends, maybe. Well, on Sundays."

"But—but—"

"Listen, Bella," Ellie finally said. "You don't want to be in the company, fine. I thought for a while maybe I didn't want to be in it, either. But that was just because my mom was pushing me so hard. Wouldn't it be pretty dumb of me to quit dance—which I love— just because my mother wants me to keep on doing it?"

"Well, but—"

"And I'm not going to quit just to keep you company," Ellie said firmly. "Although I *am* going to go home with you today, after the audition. At least your mother won't actually go berserk while I'm there."

"But what'll I do while you're auditioning?" Bella asked.

Ellie shrugged. "I don't know. Wait for me, I guess. We're here," she added as the bus squeaked to a stop. "Got everything?"

The ballet studio's waiting room was warm, noisy, and crowded. Dancers already in the company were starting to warm up; they ignored the kids who were auditioning for the first time. Lots of dancers were from different ballet schools around town, and Ellie didn't know them. There were a few boys there who were her age and some who were older. Ellie wished Bella had come too, but her friend had decided to wait at the coffee shop until the audition was over.

Ellie got in line to register. When she reached the head of the line, Ms. Hawkins automatically handed her a form to fill out; then she looked up and said, "Oh, Leticia. This came for you, dear." She handed Ellie an envelope.

Ellie took both the form and the letter and sat down on the floor. The envelope was addressed to "Leticia Elena Lane (Ellie)." Ellie ripped it open. There was a photograph enclosed, and a message:

Dear Ellie,

    Good luck! I knew you'd try out. I hope you get in. You'll go all the way if you want—I can tell. But if you don't want to, you can always be an interviewer! You're good at that, too. Here's the picture you wanted, by the way.

                    Bye!

                Anne Marie Leone

P.S. I'm having more fun already!

Ellie smiled, surprised. The famous Anne Marie had written her—*her*—just to wish her luck! She could hardly believe it.

She turned to the form Ms. Hawkins had given

her. It asked her to write down her name, address, and phone number. She wrote down "Ellie Lane"; then she underlined *Ellie*. Next, she wrote down her height and weight. Then she wrote down where she had studied ballet, dates included.

Ellie turned in the form, was given a number—27—and took her dance bag into the dressing room to change her clothes. The other girls were pretty quiet as they changed, looking sideways at one another. One girl, a little heavier than the others, left the room, and two girls giggled. Ellie tried not to think about what they would do or say when *she* left the dressing room. She pulled on the new tights her mom had bought for the audition. She tried not to think about her mother, either.

It was difficult finding the space to warm up in the waiting room, but Ellie soon staked out an area and began to stretch. She tried not to stare at anyone. She looked instead at the bits of adhesive tape stuck here and there on the gray carpet. She squinted her eyes, imagining a miniature constellation.

The thought of starting pas de deux classes—being partnered, being held and lifted by the boys stretching beside her—was exciting and scary. Well, maybe it would never happen, she thought, looking at some of the other dancers. The competition would be tough.

The audition was basically an ordinary class, Ellie kept reassuring herself, only with new kids auditioning alongside the current Philadelphia Dance Theater company members. Several adults—teachers and board members—sat in folding chairs, holding clipboards. All the dancers acted casual, but the new kids were made obvious by the numbers pinned to their leotards.

Class started at the barre, as usual, then progressed to the center of the room. Ellie lost her balance twice when turning to her right, doing pirouettes she'd done perfectly a thousand times before. She couldn't believe it.

After a while, all the girls were instructed to put on their pointe shoes. They sat scattered around the edges of the big, mirrored room while the boys stayed in the center doing tours en l'air. One new boy tripped while trying to do a double turn, but he said he was okay. Ellie felt dizzy when he stumbled. The way things were going, pretty soon it would be her turn to hit the ground.

She fumbled with the adhesive tape, her fingers feeling huge and numb as she tried to hurry. Finally—and just in time—she tucked the silky pink ribbon ends out of sight, and she was ready for the rest of the audition. Mr. Jeffries took over the class.

"And, ladies," he said.

She didn't fall, but that was just about the only bad thing that didn't happen; it was what the kids called a suicide class for Ellie. Lucky number 27!

Her ankles wobbled—look at all those judges with their clipboards! They hated her.

Her toe shoes hit the resilient floor with what sounded to Ellie like deafening clunks—that one boy was staring at her. He was probably thinking he could never lift her, not in a million years.

Ellie felt herself move across the floor while she was doing fouetté turns. You weren't supposed to move even an inch. "Pretend you're nailed to that spot," Ms. Hawkins had always said. Oh, no—she was going to crash into that high school girl. She was getting a dirty look, and no wonder.

Next came the grande allegro, usually Ellie's favorite part of any class. Sometimes she felt she was soaring when she jumped! The dancers ran diagonally across the room doing the teacher's different combinations, first in groups of three, then two at a time, then alone.

But today, Ellie had trouble even remembering Mr. Jeffries's combinations. Her mother was going to murder her when she got home, she kept thinking. If Bella's mother didn't kill her first, that is. Either way, she was doomed.

Class finished with slow turns in arabesque, in which the dancer has to make a complete slow rotation, with one foot always on the ground and the other extended high behind—all while keeping the back perfectly straight. Usually these went well for Ellie, but today—naturally—she had trouble with them. She felt her grounded foot shift and wobble. What if Bella wasn't at the coffee shop when she got out?

She felt her extended leg droop like an umbrella slowly going down, and she tried to correct herself. What if Bella's hair *never* grew back?

"And finish," Mr. Jeffries said. "You'll be notified by mail, ladies and gentlemen. Thank you."

The judges applauded as the dancers bowed and curtsied first to them, then to Mrs. Fiori. Then the dancers joined in the applause, picked up their belongings, and filed out of the room. Ellie's face burned with embarrassment as she clutched her dance bag to her chest. Could her audition have gone any worse? She was surprised the judges weren't actually hissing and booing her.

But at least she'd gone through with the audition, and at least it was over.

*I know I did the right thing, even if I don't
know how it will turn out.*

—To be continued.

12
Ellie's Head

It was late Sunday night. More than a week had
passed since the company audition. The light from a
desk lamp shone on Ellie's head as she bent over her
homework. She nibbled the end of her pen as she read
through her final interview for Ms. Yardley's English
class—the interview with herself.

THE SECRET LIFE
OF A MIDDLE SCHOOL DANCER
by Ellie Lane

*I have been taking ballet lessons for more
than half my life. I started when I was five.
Then, I only took class once a week, but
now I go at least four times a week. Next
year I will have either class or rehearsal six
days a week, because I have been invited to
join the Philadelphia Dance Theater!*

Ellie thought back to the day last week when the letter

had arrived. Her mother hadn't said anything, but it had been waiting on her bed when she got home from dance. She ripped the envelope open and spotted the one fabulous, unexpected word: "Congratulations!"

Ms. Hawkins had added a personal message at the bottom of the letter.

Leticia—or rather, Ellie—everyone has a horrific class now and then. It's about time you had one too! Now you know what auditions can be like, and that's something every gifted dancer has to find out sooner or later. Congratulations on getting in the company, dear! We have every confidence in you.

Ellie waited until dinner to tell her parents the good news. She and her mother were still acting stiff around each other, ever since their fight on Friday night. They hadn't talked about much of anything since then; instead, they'd acted extra-polite. Ellie's father had seemed to stand in the background, as though wanting to give them room to apologize.

Now, though, a smile broke through her mom's frozen expression. "Oh, that's wonderful news, sweetie," she said.

"They're lucky to have you," Ellie's father said stoutly. "If you decide to accept, that is," he added, looking at his wife. Ellie was astonished to see him wink at Mrs. Lane.

"I'm going to accept," Ellie said. "So," she added after a moment of awkward silence, "now my classes will be free, but I guess we'll have to pay for more shoes since I'll be dancing every day."

"That's okay, Ellie. Don't you worry about that," her mother said.

"Well, anyway, thanks," Ellie said awkwardly. "For everything. I know how hard you guys work, and stuff."

"We're happy to do it, sweetie. I just hope that—Oh, Ellie, I'm trying not to get too involved with this whole thing," her mother said. "It's hard, though."

"I know, Mom," Ellie said, embarrassed. "But this was my decision, and it has to be all me from now on. I mean, if I'm old enough to do this, I *have* to be the one to decide what clothes and jewelry a dancer should wear, and what food to put in my mouth when I'm away from home, and stuff like that. Not you."

Her mother tilted her head as if considering Ellie's heated words. Then she looked at her daughter and said, "I think we have to talk about that note you left the other morning."

"That's right, we do," her father said.

Ellie blushed. Were they ganging up on her, now? She wanted to forget all about the note. "What about it?" she asked, staring at her place mat.

"You wrote that I've been hurting your feelings lately," her mother said.

"Well, yeah—like when you don't listen to what I'm trying to say. And when you act like if it weren't for you, I'd go around dressing all wrong and eating all the wrong foods," Ellie said. "That's not true."

"Ellie, you're exaggerating," her father protested. "You can give your mother a little more credit than that."

They *were* ganging up on her! Ellie blushed. "Well, it sure feels like you don't listen." Her voice shook. "And it really bothers me. What are you trying to make me do? Start acting crazy, like Dawn?"

"Sweetie, no, of course not," her mother said, troubled.

"You know that's not what we want," her father said. He looked hurt.

Ellie looked at the two of them sitting there together, and she relented a little. "I know, I know," she said. "It's just . . . I think we need to listen to each other better from now on, that's all."

Ellie's parents had looked at each other, and shy smiles flickered across their faces. "No argument here," her dad said.

●

Being a dancer affects your whole body. For one thing, you start to walk like a duck! This is because of turnout. You are trained to point your toes out when you stand. That is first position, and after a few years, you don't even think about it. You just do it—all the time. Another thing dancing affects is your hair. Girl dancers have to have long hair and wear it in a bun when they dance. This leads to the nickname "bunhead," which used to bother me a whole lot.

Ellie had gone home with Bella after the audition. Mrs. Amory took one look at Bella's hair and flopped down on the sofa, speechless.

"I—I didn't go to the audition, Mother. And you can't make me!" Bella said. Then she started to cry.

Mrs. Amory held her arms out to Bella, and Bella threw herself into them. Bella sobbed, Mrs. Amory patted her on the back with a stiff, awkward hand, and Ellie edged toward the door. "But your beautiful hair," Mrs. Amory said with a gasp.

"It wasn't Ellie's idea," Bella cried.

Shut up, shut up, Ellie thought, afraid her friend would tell the whole story from beginning to end. And she had promised not to!

"Of course it wasn't, darling. But why?" Mrs. Amory asked. "Why did you do it?"

"I just don't want to be in the company. I told you and *told* you. But then you hired that coach and everything. And this was the only way—"

"You did this to yourself just to get out of auditioning?"

"Yes. You just wouldn't listen! You acted like having me in the company would be sort of a reminder of how perfect things were when you were a kid, or something. And now I can't even dance," Arabella said, breaking into fresh sobs. "All because of you."

"Bella, I think you can still take class, at least," Mrs. Amory soothed, concentrating for the moment on the last thing Bella had said. "If you want to dance,

I mean." Bella nodded, mute and miserable. "And things weren't so perfect for me, Bella," her mother continued.

"They weren't?" Bella asked.

"No—and that's one of the reasons I wanted you to have dance, so you could skip some of the awkwardness I always felt with my own body. Well," she said with a sigh, "I'll call your teacher on Monday and see if we can't work something out so you can still be in Level Six, at least. In the meantime, though, would you like me to call my hairdresser and see if he can't—um, tidy up your new haircut just a little? Maybe he can squeeze you in, later this afternoon."

"Oh, yes, *please*," Bella said.

Bella had been back in Level Six the following Monday, and she'd looked prettier than ever. "I think short hair makes your eyes look bigger," Ellie observed.

"That's what someone at school said, too," Bella replied, shaking her head experimentally. "See?" she added. "I practically don't even need to comb it, and there's no way it can get in my eyes during turns."

"I'm glad you can take class, anyway."

"Me too. I'd really hate it if I had to stop cold turkey."

Dancing also affects what you can eat. For instance, you can eat a whole bag of candy and sneak it from your parents, but you can't sneak it from your body. So you have to be the one to decide, but you can't let it make you crazy.

There are good things and bad things about being a dancer. First, the bad things. Number one: Ballet isn't fair. There has to be someplace you can take lessons, and you have to have enough money to do it. Also, if your legs end up too short, or if you don't grow enough, or if you grow too much, you probably won't ever be a professional dancer. And none of those things would be your fault.

Number two: Ballet is competitive. Of all the kids who get as far in dance as I have, maybe only one in a hundred has any chance of dancing professionally. That kind of competition can make ballet students critical and sometimes even mean. But now, I think that wanting to be the best at something can be a good quality, too. Maybe it's even a necessary quality for a dancer to have.

●

Dawn Upjohn had called that Saturday night. "So, how did it go?" she asked. "Do you think you got in?"

"I don't know," Ellie said, reluctant to tell Dawn how badly she'd done. But Dawn was going to find out anyway, the way everyone talked. "I don't think so. Most of the other kids did better. I guess it depends on who they need in the company. How are you feeling, by the way?"

"I'm okay," Dawn said abruptly. "I think I'm getting a terrible sore throat, though."

"Oh, that's too bad," Ellie said. She could almost see Dawn poking at her neck.

"Were there any guys at the audition?" Dawn asked, clearly eager to change the subject.

"Yeah," Ellie said, then she laughed. "Being partnered would have been so weird! If I got in, I mean," she added hurriedly.

"You'll get in," Dawn said, sounding a little gloomy. "I guess everyone was wondering where I was."

"Um, not really," Ellie said. No one had even mentioned Dawn; each had been too busy with her own concerns. "They were pretty quiet."

"And you didn't tell them anything about . . . you know? About what my mom thinks is wrong with me?"

"No," Ellie said.

"Well, thanks," Dawn said grudgingly. "I'm definitely auditioning in August, and I'll probably come back to class in another week or two. If my counselor says it's a good idea. And it's always kind of fun seeing if you and I can keep up with each other," she added. It sounded almost like a challenge!

"Yeah, it *is* fun," Ellie had said—and she'd meant it. It was weird, but class didn't seem the same without Dawn; Ellie guessed she was used to having her around.

Number three: Ballet takes up all your free time.

You're the one who has to give a lot of things up, and so you're the only one who should make the decision to be a dancer. For me, making that decision means I can't do other things after school next year, such as joining a club or getting a job. I will have to quit the chess club next year, for example. I already told Mr. Branowski.

And she'd told Case. "See," she tried to explain, "I was really letting him down a lot." They were standing on Ben Franklin's broad front steps after school like rocks in a stream, ignoring all the kids swirling around them.

"But how come you have to quit completely?" he asked. "Can't you still go some of the time?" He really looked upset, Ellie was surprised—and thrilled—to see.

Ellie shifted her backpack on her shoulders and shook her head. "I just can't. It wouldn't be right," she said.

But Case hadn't given up. "Well," he said, "what about if we keep on playing chess together? Whenever we can? Ned too, of course," he added hurriedly.

"Oh, yeah, Ned too," Ellie said.

"I mean, we were just starting to get good at this," Case said, a sudden grin brightening his face. "It would be kind of dumb to stop now, just when we were getting good."

But there are positive things about ballet too. Number one: It is good exercise. Even if you don't want to do it for a living, you can take class, no matter how old you are. This one lady at our studio is seventy, and she says if she does her stretching exercises every day, there will never be a day she can't do them.

Number two: Ballet has a wonderful history. Also, I like to think of all the people who are taking class just like I do, everywhere in the world. We are all part of that tradition.

Number three: Ballet is beautiful. Not only is it beautiful to watch, it's beautiful to do. Your body and your mind have to work together, and when they mix just right with the piano music, you feel very peaceful. But ballet is also exciting.

Well, it is kind of hard to explain, but I hope this article has told you a little bit about my secret life as a middle school dancer.

I know that many of you have secret lives too, with music, acting, sports, or art. And so you know how I feel—that no matter what else happens in my life, I'm proud to be a bunhead!